HOOKER

PRESS

Other Books published by **j**-Press

Where Evil Hides, by Dean Hovey, 2001

The Nisei Soldier: Historical Essays on WWII and the Korean War, by Edwin M. Nakasone, 1999

A Dream for Gilberto: An Immigrant Family's Struggle to Become American, by Billie Young, 1999

Film & Art, by Bruce H. Hinrichs, 2000

Mind as Mosaic:the robot in the Machine by Bruce H. Hinrichs, 2000

Come & Dine, by Abigail Brown Collins, 2001

Deja Vu and the Phone Sex Queen by Michael McIrvin, 2001

j-Press books may be ordered directly on-line at www.jpresspublishing.com, by phone at 888-407-1723, or by mail at **j**-Press Publishing, 4796 N. 126th St., White Bear Lake, MN 55110

Our books are also available in bookstores throughout the U.S. and from most on-line bookstores.

HOOKER

By

DEAN HOVEY

j-Press Publishing
4796 N. 126th St.
White Bear Lake, MN 55110

j-Press Publishing
4796 N. 126th St.
White Bear Lake, MN 55110
Phone: 1-888-407-1723

Visit the **j**-Press website at http://www.jpresspublishing.com

First printing, June 2002
Printed in the United States of America.
06 05 04 03 02   6 5 4 3 2 1

Publisher's Cataloging in Publication Data

Hovey, Dean L.
Hooker / Dean L. Hovey.
261 p.; cm.
ISBN 1-930922-03-5
1. Detective and mystery stories.
2. Minnesota—Fiction.
3. Pine County (Minn.)—Fiction.
I. Title.

Library of Congress Control Number: 2002101727

This book is dedicated to Julie

*I have to acknowledge the assistance of a number of people who have helped me with detail, critical review, and support. Dennis Arnold's decades in rural law enforcement have been critical to making sure "the police stuff" is correct. Frannie Brozo, Lynn Hovey, Natalie Lund, Mike Westfall, Paul Martin, Laurie Hoversten, and Bil (with one L) Brummund have all been proofreaders, friends, and critics. Sid Jackson, from **j**-Press, has challenged me to create the best books that I am capable of writing. Robert G. Smith braved the winds of a Minnesota October to take great publicity photos. Jim Hansen helped with a software conversion and offered solace.*

Many thanks to the members of the literary community, who have been tremendously supportive. With encouragement from dozens of authors, critics, booksellers, libraries, and readers, it has been difficult not to spend my evenings in front of the computer dreaming up new Pine County crimes.

HOOKER

Chapter 1

"I think I figured it out," the female voice on the phone whispered. Ann Olsen rubbed the sleep from her eyes. She couldn't quite place the voice. The glowing numerals on the alarm clock said it was 11:00 p.m.

"Is that you, Jean?"

"I didn't wake Eric, did I?"

"No," Ann replied, "he's back on midnight shift."

"Ann ... I've decided to call the guy to tell him what I'm gonna do."

"Are you sure that's a good idea?" Ann asked.

"No. I don't know how he'll take it. But, I've got to do it. I've got to get on with my life."

"Are you going to tell me who *he* is? You've been keeping this from me for months."

"Maybe, after it's settled, but not now. You understand, don't you?"

"I know it's a secret," Ann conceded, "but I'm dying to know all the details."

"Maybe tomorrow. After I talk to him. Okay?"

" Okay. Sure. Call me in the morning."

Jean Oinen dialed another number and waited for four rings before a groggy, male voice answered.

"Hullo?"

"This is Jean. I've made a big decision about something. Can you come over tonight?"

"What?" The man asked in confusion. "A decision about what?"

"Just come over. I can't tell you over the phone."

"What the hell time is it?"

Jean looked at the clock on her desk. "It's eleven-forty-five."

"You want me to come over *now*?"

"Not right now. I'm free at ..." she paused and looked at her Franklin planner, "say, one-thirty."

"You want me to come over at one-thirty, in the morning, because you've made a decision? C'mon, Jean! What's so important it can't wait 'til tomorrow?"

"Look, I'm just going to drive down and sit in the office until you can see me."

"Oh, good God!" he growled. "Okay. Okay. I'll be over at one-thirty, but this better be good."

Chapter 2

W hat's the matter?" Vera Youngquist was reaching for her glasses to see what had caused her husband to sit bolt upright in bed. The digital alarm clock said 2:16 a.m.

"Didn't you hear it?" Ed Youngquist sat up on the side of the bed and listened. Only a few moments passed when he heard the sound again. "There! Did you hear that?" He rose stiffly, then went to the window. He spread the mini-blinds a fraction of an inch and peered into the night.

"I didn't hear anything. What do you think you heard?" Vera pulled herself up and sat resting against the headboard of the bed.

"Sounded like a scream. It was cut short."

Through the crack in the blinds Vera could see the lights in the neighboring mobile home on the lot only thirty feet away. "Ed, you're hearing things. You're just trying to get a look at that young woman again. You're a lecherous old man, Ed Youngquist!"

In the darkness of the bedroom, Vera couldn't see the blood rush to Ed's face. She had hit closer to the mark than she realized. On more than one occasion he'd gotten a glimpse of the young female neighbor entertaining a male visitor in her bedroom. Ed had found himself peeking through their bedroom window to the trailer across the way more frequently than he wanted to admit, and certainly more often than he wanted Vera to know about. Over the weeks and months there had been many male visitors, and their neighbor didn't seem too concerned about pulling the shades while she and her partners enjoyed their sexual gymnastics.

"I'm just checking to make sure everything is okay, Vera, you know that," Ed said, gruffly. He let the blinds slide together and walked back to the bed.

"I know you're a dirty old snoop!" Vera said. "You'd better get some sleep."

Ed Youngquist, owner of the trailer park, climbed back into bed, but couldn't fall asleep. He tossed and turned, and listened. Just as he was dozing off, he was awakened again. He sat up in bed, listening. Vera turned over, moaning slightly.

"Did you hear that? I think I heard a door slam." Ed was out of bed and at the window again. "Hey! There's a dog scratching at something out there. I'm going to turn on the porch light."

Vera raised up on one elbow and looked at the clock. It was 3:32 a.m. She wondered if Ed had been asleep yet. Through the blinds she saw their porch light come on.

Vera took the chenille robe from the chair next to the bed. She was pulling it on when she heard their front door open and the screened door slam shut. She walked to the kitchen and looked out at the small patio that separated the two mobile homes. Their neighbor's door was open and Ed was squatting down, looking at something on the ground, as the dog scurried around, sniffing.

Ed stood up and walked back to the door. Vera held it open for him. He turned on the kitchen light and looked at his hand. Across the index finger he saw a smear of dark red. "Hey, that's blood!," he exclaimed. "There's blood coming out of Jeanie's trailer. I'm going to call the sheriff."

Chapter 3

The phone jarred Sally Williams from her sleep. She fumbled with the receiver for a second before getting it to her ear. "Hello?"

"Sorry to wake you, Sally; this is dispatch. I need to talk to Dan."

"Oh, okay. Hang on." Sally reached for the switch on the nightlight. Beside her, Dan Williams was beginning to stir from a deep sleep.

"Mister Chief Investigator, dispatch wants you," said Sally.

Williams tried to rub the sleep from his eyes as he took the receiver. "Yeah. What's up?" He pulled himself into a sitting position, fully awake now. Sally had always marveled at his ability to go from a deep sleep to a rational cop in a matter of seconds.

"Dan, Sandy Maki responded to a call from the trailer court in Sturgeon Lake. Ed Youngquist reported hearing a scream. Sandy says that the front door to the neighbor's trailer was open, and that there's lots of blood inside. There's no sign of the neighbor. They're looking for her now."

"Okay. Tell Sandy I'll be there in twenty minutes."

He pressed the button and released it, then dialed the home number of the St. Louis County medical examiner, which he knew from memory. The phone was answered on the fourth ring.

"Tony? This is Dan Williams. I've got a crime scene here. Can you come down and take a look?"

There was a pause as Tony Oresek, M.E., reached for his glasses. "Well, of course, Dan! Of course! You know it's my favorite thing to do at … four in the morning. Is it okay if I bring Eddie along? We might as well spoil his night's sleep, too."

"Sure," said Williams. "The more the merrier as far as I'm concerned. The call came from the mobile-home park in Sturgeon Lake, east of the freeway. Go to the lake and turn right. When you get to all the flashing lights, you'll be there."

Sally watched as Dan rolled out of bed, pulled on a pair of jeans and a flannel shirt. "What's the deal?" she asked.

"Don't know, yet. Missing person, possibly foul play. I'll let you know as soon as I can."

Sally plopped back down on the bed and pulled the covers to her chin. "Okay, but don't make it too soon. I'm sleeping in this morning."

. . .

Within three minutes Dan was in the brown Crown Victoria, racing toward the village of Sturgeon Lake, just a few miles from his home. He drove past the sleeping houses and businesses without a siren, then turned it on as he sped toward I-35, a mile east of the downtown area. A few blocks past the interstate, he turned down the road leading to the trailer park, situated by the lake. Before he'd traveled a hundred yards, he could see three sets of flashing red and blue lights. When he reached the mobile home park, he saw two Pine County squads, flanked by one highway patrol squad. He exited from his own vehicle and walked between the cars toward the lighted courtyard that was congested with a dozen people in bathrobes and slippers. Sandy Maki waved him to the front of a mobile home. Yellow crime scene tape had already cordoned off the area between the trailer house and the neighboring trailers.

"Hi, Sandy. What have we got?"

"Hi, Dan. Got a call from Ed Youngquist, … " he gestured toward a portly, older man in a robe, who was restraining a small dog on a leash, "… said he'd heard a scream earlier this evening, but said he didn't see anything. Later, he heard a door slam and some scraping noises. He went outside and found blood on the patio between his trailer and the neighboring trailer. The neighbor's front door was open. That's when he called."

"Okay, Sandy. Let's have a look."

They ducked under the yellow tape and Sandy led Dan toward the trailer with the open door. "I've tried to be real careful," Sandy said, "but I did touch a couple of door knobs."

They opened the screen door and walked onto the linoleum entryway. The stench of blood permeated the air. Dan looked down at the brown sticky ooze that smeared the linoleum. Sandy gestured down the hallway and took a deep gulp of air.

"There's blood all down the hall, too. Some in the bedroom

and the bathroom's ... well, it's real bad."

Williams walked down the hall toward the rear of the trailer. When he got to the bathroom, he realized that Maki was not following him. He turned back and saw Maki facing the other way with his hands on his hips, breathing deeply.

The bathroom floor was splashed with the brown ooze and the bathtub was half full of a disgusting mixture of blood and water. The water diluted the upper layer of blood so that it took on a redder appearance than normal. The bottom layer was rusty-brown. Dan turned his attention to the remaining part of the trailer.

There was a faint brown stain running the length of the hallway carpeting from the back room, which Williams assumed to be the bedroom. Williams made his way down the hall and entered the bedroom. On the bed, the white sheets showed a small reddish-brown stain. There was a smear where the body had apparently been dragged off the bed and onto the floor.

Williams walked back to Maki. "Does the trail go outside too?"

"Yeah," Maki said, "but we lost it when it hit the gravel. Maybe we'll be able to see it better in the daylight."

"Let's take a look," Dan said.

They crossed the narrow courtyard and Maki showed Dan where the trail apparently ended. Williams knelt down on the ground and rubbed his finger in the dirt. "Sandy," he said, looking up, "can you see if anyone has a gas lantern we could borrow?" He motioned to the crowd of onlookers beyond the police line.

"Sure," said Sandy, "I'll check." He trotted off, returning

shortly with a Coleman gas lantern with both wicks blazing. It shed an eerie, blue-white glow on the ground. Williams held it chest high and started to follow the sparkling trail on the road.

"Is that blood?" Maki asked.

"An old deer poacher's trick," Dan replied. "There's apparently a chemical interaction between the gas light and the hemoglobin in fresh blood. The blood really sparkles when you're on a fresh trail." They followed the trail of twinkling spots and streaks between some mobile homes, across the road and to the edge of the lake.

"Looks like they went swimming, or else left by boat." Dan handed the lantern to Maki. "Mark this trail with spray paint so we can find it in the morning. Then take a drive around the shore. Check the public-access boat launches for blood and fresh tire tracks."

. . .

Back at the trailer park, Williams sought out Ed and Vera Youngquist. He was directed to their trailer by a neighbor, and ducked under the crime-scene tape to knock on the door. Ed Youngquist answered.

"Mr. Youngquist. I'm Dan Williams, the investigator from the Pine County sheriff's department. I would like to ask you a few questions."

"Oh, my. Yes. Yes. Please come in."

Ed ushered Williams into the tiny dining area off the kitchen. The man appeared to be in his seventies, his age accentuated by his gray beard stubble and too little sleep. He was six-inches shorter than Dan, and appeared to stretch the limits of his bathrobe's girth.

In the air was the smell of fresh coffee brewing. As the two men sat down at the dining table, Vera, short and petite, pulled the urn from under the Mr. Coffee machine. She carried three mugs in one hand and the coffeepot in the other. Without asking, she poured a mug for each of them.

Dan smiled inwardly at the typical Scandinavian hospitality. In Pine County, Minnesota, no one asked if you drank coffee. No one offered herbal tea. You got a cup of medium-strong coffee and were expected to drink it. Sugar and cream were optional.

Ed Youngquist pulled a spoon from a mug in the center of the table and dumped two rounded teaspoons of sugar into the cup and stirred. Vera added half-n-half to her coffee, directly from the carton. Dan refused both and savored the coffee, looking forward to a rush that would bring him fully awake.

"It was real strange," Ed said without prompting. "I woke up about two. I thought I'd heard a scream. I looked out the window and all the lights were blazing at Jeanie's, but I didn't see anything going on."

"It was two-sixteen," Vera corrected, "and he peeked between the blinds to try and catch another glimpse of Jeanie romping around naked with one of her friends." The word *friends* dripped with sarcasm. Ed Youngquist's face turned a bright red.

"I take it 'Jeanie' is your missing neighbor? And that she had a number of friends that visited?" Williams directed his questions at Vera.

"Oh, you betcha! She had *lots* of friends, I can tell you.

Sometimes she had two or three a night! They'd come and go at all hours. They'd cavort and holler and laugh. As soon as one left, a new one would show up and it would start all over."

Ed's face had turned back to something of its normal color and he had apparently regained most of his composure. "Jeanie is just a fun-loving girl, Sheriff, with lots of boyfriends. You and I had a little fun in our own day, too, eh?" He winked at Williams.

"I hope you didn't have your fun with married women, Ed Youngquist!" Vera said emphatically, "and if you did, I hope you didn't charge them for the pleasure."

Ed rolled his eyes for Dan's benefit. "If I told you once, I told you a hundred times; she don't charge 'em. She's just a fun-lovin' gal. She ain't no prostitute!"

"Hold it, folks!" Dan said, holding a hand in the air for effect. "I just want to know what facts you can tell me about Jeanie. I don't want a fight here and I don't want rumors. Let's start with Jeanie's last name."

Ed jumped in. "Oinen." He pronounced it "Weenan." "I think She'd been living with her dad in Moose Lake until she moved here about three years ago." He looked at Vera triumphantly, as if he'd been quicker at answering a game-show question and had won big bucks.

"She lived by herself?" Dan asked. "No roommates?"

"It's tough to have roommates when you do so much entertaining," Vera snorted. She stared balefully at Ed.

"Any family that came to visit regularly?" asked Williams.

"No," Ed replied. "Mainly just her men friends. Some blonde girl used to visit once in awhile, in the afternoons. Rumor is that

Jeanie's father threw her out of their trailer in Moose Lake."

"Do you know who was over tonight?"

"I never pay any attention," said Vera, "but Ed spends half his life peeking out between the blinds to try and catch another glimpse of bare titty."

Ed looked at Williams in exasperation. "That's not the truth, Sheriff! As owner and manager I have to check the weather, I check to make sure the dogs are not getting into the garbage … well, you know, I have to take care of everything."

"Uh huh! And while you're at it you check to see if Jeanie's got a tan line," said Vera, "and if there are any bare butts showing under the edge of the window shade. Uh huh."

Ed Youngquist started to turn bright red again, and Williams surmised that there might be more than a hint of truth to Vera's accusations.

Dan repeated the question. "But do you know who was over tonight?"

Ed folded his arms across his ample belly and scowled at Vera. "No! We don't." He turned back to Williams with a see-what-I-have-to-put-up-with look.

"How about you, Vera?" asked Dan, ignoring Ed's "we" reference.

Vera, belying the rough-edged character she'd exhibited so far, began to fidget. "I'm not a gossip. I'd just as soon not say who I saw, Sheriff Williams."

"Mrs. Youngquist, this isn't a matter of gossip," Dan admonished. "We're investigating a possible murder. This is very important. Did you see someone you could identify at Jean's?"

"One, I know," Vera said. "Harry Nord, the first one, was

walking out of Jeanie's when I let the dog out at eight-thirty. He looked pretty pleased with himself. The other one ... well, I've only seen his picture, but I know his name: Orrin Petrich ... the senator ... looks a lot older than his picture. He was knocking at the door when I checked the temperature at eleven and he didn't look too happy."

Williams scribbled the names of the local businessman and the state senator in a notebook. Both were probably married men. He frowned at the thought of the ripples that this incident might send through the community.

"Are they regular visitors?"

"I've seen a lot of different men over there," said Vera. "I've never seen Petrich before, but Nord comes and goes. Ed has probably seen more'n I have."

Ed shook his head. "I don't keep track of 'em," he said, looking at Vera defiantly. "It's no business of mine. There's a lot of people who enjoy a party with Jeanie. She's fun. She takes a man's mind off things." Then, quickly, he said ,"At least, that's what you hear."

Fortunately, before Vera could jump on Ed again, there was a knock at the door and Ed Youngquist quickly answered it. It was Sandy Maki.

"Mr. Youngquist, could you tell Undersheriff Williams that the medical examiner is here, from Duluth?"

Dan rose from his chair and walked to the door. "I'll be out in a second, Sandy. Show him the trailer." He turned back to the Youngquists. "Is there anything else that you can tell me that might help with the investigation?"

Ed shook his head. Vera looked Dan in the eye. "You got one

hell of a chore, Sheriff Williams, if you ask me. Jeanie has been entertaining half the businessmen in Pine and Carlton Counties, and I 'spect there are a lot of people who would just as soon not have everyone know about it."

Chapter 4

Williams walked into the entryway of the Oinen trailer and heard voices from the bathroom. He walked down the hall and looked around the corner at Tony Oresek and his assistant, Eddie Paulson. They were leaning over the edge of the tub, gently stirring the water.

"Glad you could make it," Dan said.

They looked up. "Hell of a mess here," Oresek, the medical examiner said. "Looks like somebody tried to dump a lot of blood into the drain, but it clotted and plugged the trap. Then that person must have run the water in on top to try and flush it down, but all it did was dilute it."

"I assume that it's human blood?" Williams thought it was necessary to ask the obvious question.

"Officially, I can't say until we look at a sample under the microscope," Eddie said, holding up a small vial with a label marked with his scribbled handwriting. "Unofficially, it smells human."

"Are we searching for a body," Dan asked, "or a very badly wounded person?"

Oresek considered the tub and said, "If this all came from one person, dead. Looks like an exsanguinating wound. Bled the victim dry. There must be five or six pints in the tub. Plus whatever drained before plugging, and what's smeared in the hallway."

Williams backed out of the bathroom and walked to the tiny bedroom. "It looks like it started here and the body was dragged to the bathroom." Rugs that appeared to belong on the floor near the bed, were heaped close to the door. One had a brown stain.

Oresek scanned the scene. "Hardly any blood here. The victim didn't have an arterial wound at this point ... there's not enough volume, and little sign of a struggle. There aren't any blood-spatter patterns on the walls or bedding, either, so it wasn't a bludgeoning. Probably a blow to the head, and then the murderer dragged the unconscious victim to the tub and opened a major blood vessel there. Either the murderer is very skilled in anatomy, or very lucky."

"The neighbor said he thought he heard a scream that was cut short."

Oresek shrugged. "Could have been a head blow that knocked her unconscious, or a slash through the trachea that wasn't deep enough to catch a vessel. No, on second thought, it couldn't have been a slashed trachea. The victim would have been conscious and struggling. There would be more of a mess. I'll stick with a blow to the head and an unconscious victim."

Oresek leaned down to examine the smears of blood on the sheets and followed them to the head of the bed. He pointed to a spot on the headboard.

"There are a couple long hairs stuck on the wood here. It appears that someone may have struck his or her head. If we ever recover a body, we may find a contusion that matches."

Eddie Paulson removed the hairs with a forceps and placed them in an evidence bag.

Oresek added, "If the contusion is deep enough, it may explain the scream being cut short. The victim may have been unconscious at that point."

Williams shook his head in admiration. He didn't even have a body yet but already the ME had given him a much clearer picture.

"Okay, Tony. Let me know when you're finished here and I'll let the evidence team in to dust for prints."

Chapter 5

On the drive to the courthouse, Williams pondered the bits of information he'd gleaned from the medical examiner, the Youngquists, and the crime scene. In his office, he called the Moose Lake police and spoke with the dispatcher. The dispatcher told him that he would call the officers on duty to see if anyone knew the Oinens.

Williams was thinking about the blood trail to the lake and was trying to decide about getting some divers out in the morning when the phone rang. "Williams."

"Hi, Dan. Mike Ronning here. The dispatcher said you wanted to talk about the Oinens?"

"Yeah, Mike. Can you help?"

" We have several Oinen families in the area. Which ones are you interested in?"

"Some folks in Sturgeon Lake said that Jeanie Oinen used to live with her father in town until about three or four years ago."

"Uh huh. Well, she didn't move out," Ronning said. "Her father threw her out. Topped the gossip around here for awhile. What do you need to know?"

"To start with, a little background. What's the father's name?"

"Elmer. He still lives in the trailer they shared on the hill behind the Chev dealer, just west of downtown. A kinda quiet guy. Works in town as a mechanic."

"What was the big blow up?"

The officer chuckled. "We got a call about a domestic at three in the afternoon. When our officer arrived he found the daughter, Jean, sitting in the yard crying. The old man was in the trailer and every once in awhile something would come flying out the door. The officer said that there was a pile of clothes and a few pieces of furniture in the yard when he arrived."

"Why did he throw her out?" Dan asked.

"He came home from work early, caught her in the sack with a local guy. That ticked him off pretty good, but when the guy tried to pay her for the services rendered, her pop hit the ceiling. He called her a whore and started throwing her stuff out in the yard."

"Any physical abuse involved?"

"Apparently not," Ronning replied, "just a lot of yelling and crying. The officer took Jean into town and called social services. They set her up with a motel room for the night and eventually she moved to the trailer down by Sturgeon Lake. I can't say if there was any clientele, or if they followed her there. But the rumor mill says that there are several married fellas who go down to Mister Ed's Inn for a beer once in awhile, and never show up in the bar. This is all rumor, but I hear Ed tells the wives the guy just left, then he calls Jean's place to send the warning. Did you pick her up for prostitution?"

"No," Dan replied, "I guess our grapevine isn't good enough

to pick up on things like that. There was an assault at Jean's trailer and we're following up on it."

"Good luck. If there's anything else that I can do to help, feel free to call."

"Do you know the address of Elmer Oinen's trailer?" Dan asked.

"He's got a post-office box in town, but his is the fourth trailer on the right as you enter the trailer park. It's an older, green Roycraft. He drives a blue and white Blazer."

"Thanks, Mike." Dan hesitated, then asked, "Do we have any other Pine County prostitutes I should know about?"

"Not that I can think of," Ronning replied, "but I'll keep my ears open."

. . .

Williams was in Moose Lake at 5:30 a.m. He drove down a deserted Highway 61. Only a few of the houses he passed had lights on. He passed the Ford and Chevy dealers and the two restaurants, then turned left at the traffic light. At the top of the hill, he turned into the trailer park and wound his way to the Roycraft. The trailer was dark. A Blazer sat under a carport alongside the entrance door. Williams got out of his car, walked over to the Blazer and put his hand on the hood. It was cold. "Hasn't been driven for at least two or three hours," he said to himself. A layer of frost coated the windshield. If Elmer Oinen was home, he had probably just dropped off the list of top suspects.

A few knocks on the door brought a stir from inside and a

tired face peeked at Dan from behind the door. The face was heavily creased and covered with gray whiskers. Dan's first impression was that he'd seen Elmer in a bar somewhere.

"Elmer Oinen?" The man grunted in response to the question.

"I'm Dan Williams from the Pine County sheriff's department. Could I come in and ask you a few questions?" Dan flashed his badge at the man, who squinted briefly at it, then opened the door.

"Come on in, but I sure don't know what I can do for you at this hour of the morning that I couldn't do later."

The inside of the trailer was definitely a man's world. Greasy uniform shirts and pants lay over the back of the couch and chairs. The sink was full of dirty dishes and the living room was littered with more dirty dishes and beer cans. The odor of rotten food lay heavily in the air. Williams found an empty chair at the kitchen table and sat down. The other chairs either appeared broken or were supporting greasy car parts.

"Mr. Oinen, sorry to get you up so early but we've had a little incident and I have reason to believe you might be able to help me, if you don't mind."

"Well, it must be important to get a man up this early," Oinen said with obvious irritation.

"This won't take long, Mr. Oinen. Have you been home all night?"

Oinen shrugged. "I got home early. I don't socialize much. Went to bed 'bout nine and slept until you showed up and rousted me out. Why'd ya ask?"

"There's been an incident at your daughter's trailer in Sturgeon Lake last night. We're trying to figure out exactly just what happened and who might have been involved."

"I can't help you. I haven't seen Jeanie since …" the old man's eyes rolled back and he stared at the ceiling " ... she moved out. We aren't, what you'd call, on speaking terms."

"So you haven't seen her at all in awhile?"

The old man shook his head. "Several years. I got nothing to say to her."

"Do you have any idea where she might go if she was in trouble?"

"Someone to turn to if she needed help?" Oinen looked puzzled, then he shook his head.

"Who her closest friends might be?" asked Williams.

Again, Oinen shook his head.

Williams paused for a moment, looking at the old man, attempting to read any telltale signs. "Mr. Oinen, a very brutal attack on someone took place in Jeanie's trailer last night. Someone was hurt very badly. She wasn't around when we answered the call, and we're not sure what her involvement might be."

The old man looked at Dan with some concern for a moment, then shrugged. "I don't consider her my daughter no more. She did some pretty bad stuff and I don't cotton to that kind of thing. She left and I said good riddance. I hope she's okay, but I really can't be of any help."

The old man seemed truthful. Williams thought he could read it in his eyes. There was bitterness, and a hint of sorrow in his words.

Williams rose from the chair. "Again, sorry to drag you out of bed so early, Mr. Oinen. If you hear anything from Jeanie, or think of anything, please give me a call." He handed a business card to the old man.

At the door, Williams hesitated for a second. "If we hear something, would you like to know?"

The old face was blank, then Elmer shrugged. "Yeah. I guess so."

Williams let himself out, got in his squad, and drove back to the highway. Dick's Cafe was just opening, so he pulled into the lot and ordered a stack of pancakes and a cup of coffee. The thirty-something waitress smiled pleasantly and walked off with his order. He gazed at a picture of the Moose Lake girls state championship softball team, mounted on the knotty-pine paneling above the booth, and wondered if Jean Oinen had ever been an athlete. It appeared she wouldn't have had much encouragement or support from home.

. . .

After breakfast, Dan stopped in the restaurant breezeway and looked up Harry Nord's phone number. He didn't recognize the street name, so he dialed the number from the cell phone in his car and waited. A female voice answered the phone.

"Hello?"

"Is Harry Nord there, please?"

"Just a second." The voice sounded amazingly cheery for so early in the morning. In a minute, Harry was on the line.

"Mr. Nord, this is Dan Williams from the Pine County sheriff's department. I was wondering if we could talk somewhere for a few minutes?"

There was a long pause. "I guess so," Nord said. "What's this about?"

"Jean Oinen. You know her, don't you?"

There was silence for longer than a moment, then Nord's voice dropped to a near whisper. "Is this some kind of a joke? What are you trying to pull here?"

"I'm dead serious, Mr. Nord. I can come by your house, if you'd like."

Again, silence, then some muffled talking in the background, like Nord had a hand over the receiver. "Where are you now?"

"I'm sitting in my car outside Dick's restaurant."

Muffled talk again, then, "All right. I'll be there in five minutes. No, wait a minute, we can't talk there ... hang on just a second ... okay, I can meet you in the park, by the beach. Go straight down the road between the liquor store and the Amoco station and I'll be there."

The line went dead.

. . .

Williams went back into Dick's, ordered coffee in a Styrofoam cup and a roll of Tums. He drove the six blocks to the park. Nord's car wasn't there. He waited in the brown, unmarked squad for about two minutes until a yellow Buick pulled into the lot. Nord exited his car, looked around three or four times, then walked to the passenger side of the squad. Williams motioned him in.

Harry Nord was a middle-aged man who hadn't missed many meals. He didn't close the zipper on his light jacket and several of the shirt buttons strained against the cloth as he settled into the seat next to Dan. He looked nervously at Williams.

"Mr. Nord? I'm Dan Williams, undersheriff for Pine County."

"Uh huh. I know, Sheriff. What's this about?"

"What can you tell me about Jean Oinen?"

Nord hesitated. He was obviously agitated. "I'm not sure what you mean, Sheriff. Has something happened to Jean?"

Williams ignored the question. "You were seen at her trailer in Sturgeon Lake last night, Mr. Nord. Can you tell me what you were doing there?"

"Am I in some sort of trouble?" Nord asked. "Is this an arrest?"

"That depends on what you can tell me about your relationship with Miss Oinen." Williams took a sip from his coffee cup and waited.

"Did you say that someone saw me there last night? I can't remember if I was there or not, to tell you the truth."

"Yes. We have an eyewitness who says you were there about eight-thirty last night."

"Are you sure it was me they saw? It may have been someone else." Nord was probing, trying to establish his exact situation.

"Mr. Nord, if you haven't done anything illegal then you shouldn't have anything to fear. But if we find out you're lying, then you certainly could be in very deep trouble. Even if you *have* done something, it's best if you tell us. Things will go much easier for you."

"Has something happened to Jean, Sheriff? I'd just like to know what this is all about."

"We don't know, yet. Something may have happened. That's

what we're trying to find out. Were you there last night?"

Nord hesitated again, this time so long that the situation became awkward. Then he said, "Well, I am remembering, now. Yes, it was last night. I was thinking it was another night. Funny, how sometimes I get events jumbled up. You know. Does that ever happen to you, Sheriff?"

"What time did you leave?"

Nord sank a little deeper in the seat. "About nine-thirty, I'd say."

"How was Jean when you left?"

"She was just fine," Nord said. "We talked for a few minutes while we washed up the dishes. Then I left."

"There was a disturbance at the trailer later. We're trying to figure out what happened. Did you see anyone else around when you left?"

"No. I didn't see anyone when I drove off."

"What is the nature of your relationship with Jean?"

"We're just friends."

"I don't think so, Mr. Nord. We have a pretty good idea what Jean Oinen is doing. My guess is, you're no different from the others. Do you visit her often?"

"Dammit, Sheriff! I *would* like to know what this has to do with me. I don't think that is anyone else's concern."

"Where do you work, Harry? Aren't you employed at the high school?"

Nord just stared out the windshield of the car.

"What do you do there?" Dan asked. "Teacher? Librarian? Janitor?"

Nord relented. "I'm a teacher at the elementary school. Why?"

"If I can't get some good information about what was going on in Jean's trailer, I'm going to have to wander all over and stir up all kinds of people by asking lots of questions. I'd hate for the school board to get wind of this." Williams took another sip of coffee and stared out the windshield.

"On the other hand," Dan went on, "if you can give me some information that will help clear up some questions, the school board may never hear a word."

Nord was silent again, staring out the window. Williams continued to sip at his coffee.

"You're blackmailing me," Nord said, after a few moments. "Either I talk, or you sell me down the river with the school board. Is that the scenario?"

"I don't blackmail and I don't threaten, Mr. Nord. I conduct an investigation, and I just explained what the investigation may entail. If you find that threatening, it is not my problem. Law-abiding citizens usually don't have anything to fear from an investigation."

Nord gave Williams a look of disgust. "Okay, Sheriff. If that's the way it is. Just exactly what do you want to know?"

Chapter 6

Harry Nord slid farther down in the seat of the squad car and rubbed his hands over his face as Dan pulled out a small notebook. "Where do you want me to start?"

"You are one of Jean Oinen's clients, are you not?"

"Yes."

"How does one become one of Jean's clients?"

"It's a business, run strictly by referral. If someone didn't refer you, you were not welcomed as a guest."

"Who referred you?"

A pained expression crossed Nord's face, but he saw no escape. "Pat, at the five-and-dime store. He's been visiting Jeanie since she lived in the trailer park. I've only known her for a couple of years."

"Do you know who the other regulars are?"

"Aw, crap, Sheriff! My ass will be grass if I start throwing out names. Don't make me do this. Can't you go about this some other way?"

"Sure," Dan replied, zeroing in. He was beginning to get tired of Nord's evasiveness. "I can start asking everyone in town until I collect a list. That'll be real discreet, won't it?"

"Aw, shit! I don't know them all. Some are from Kettle River and Hinckley. I know about George, from the Sturgeon Lake General Store. The Doc, from Fond du Lac, has been there a couple of times. That's who Jeanie visited when someone brought a dose of clap to the group a year ago, July. There are a couple more guys. They should all be in Jeanie's appointment book."

"She kept an appointment book?" Dan asked, as he wrote "clap" in his notes.

"Sure. She had a schedule, carefully planned so we never ran into each other. We'd be there at our appointed time, have a little party, with maybe a few drinks. Then we'd take a roll in the sack, clean up, and help her wash and dry the dishes. Then we were off at our appointed time. It was like a well-oiled machine and Jeanie was the head operator."

"So you never saw who came after you?"

"Almost never. One time some political asshole showed up early and made a fuss. He left me with the impression that he felt he could come and go as he liked and that no one else was important. Jeanie chewed him out and he went and sat in his car until I left."

"Who was he?"

"I don't know. The way Jeanie talked about him made me think he was some sort of elected official, like maybe a county commissioner or legislator. She said she wished he'd never been referred."

"What did she charge?"

"It was never discussed," Nord said. "She had a little cedar box that sat on the table by the door. As I went out I'd drop money in it. She never complained about the money, or said it was too little. It was like she didn't really want the money. Like it was dirty somehow. I'd usually put in forty or fifty bucks. But I'd see fives and hundreds in there sometimes."

Nord turned and faced Williams. "I'm really not a bad guy. I love my wife. It's just that Jeanie made it so easy. It's all harmless, anyway, and I can afford it. I spend a lot less than some drop at the casino. It takes a lot of hassle and pressure out of my marriage."

Dan was trying hard not to show his disgust for this fellow. "It's not harmless anymore, Mr. Nord," he said. "We think that someone may have been killed in Jean's trailer last night."

"My God!" Nord sank even lower in his seat until his knees were resting against the dash. "What a mess!" Suddenly, he sat up. "Is Jeanie okay?"

"We don't know. We can't find her. The reports we have so far indicate she may be the victim. Do you know of anywhere she might hide if she were afraid or in trouble? Maybe somewhere she might run if she was scared or hurt?"

Nord thought for a moment. "I think the trailer was the center of her universe," he said, finally. "She talked about getting a nice house on a lake, but for now the trailer was it. I don't think that she even left to buy groceries. I think she had them delivered."

"Do you know if Jean kept a diary?"

"No. I don't think so. What I saw was an appointment book. She joked that it was the same kind that the executives used. She called it some kind of a planner—Jefferson planner? No,

Franklin planner. It had all her appointments in it. She used it to plan her whole life. If you can lay a hand on that, you'd have all the names of the clients, and maybe even the name of the last person there last night."

"Where'd she keep it?" Dan asked.

"She kept it in a little secretary desk in the bedroom. It was always in the drawer."

"You have anything else you can tell me, Mr. Nord?"

"No. That's it."

"Okay. I guess that's all for now." Dan pulled a business card from his pocket and handed it to him. "If you can think of anything else pertinent to the investigation, or if you hear from Jean, please give me a call."

Chapter 7

"Senator, there's a phone call from the Pine County sheriff's department on line two. Do you want to take it?"

Orrin Petrich peered over the top of his *Wall Street Journal* at the young receptionist peeking around the edge of his office door. He didn't like interruptions to his schedule. Right then, the schedule called for him to drink coffee and check his investments until his first committee meeting of the morning, at ten.

"Who did you say? A sheriff?" Petrich asked, his irritation quite visible.

"From Pine County, sir."

Petrich thought for a moment, trying to recall the name. "Oh, okay. I'll take it." He leaned forward and set the newspaper on the desktop while he stared at the flashing light on the phone. "I wonder what the hell John Sepanen wants from me?" he said to himself. "Hello, John. You need another campaign contribution already? I thought you just got re-elected?" Petrich put a little chuckle at the end of the comment to help lend an air of familiarity.

"Senator Petrich, this is Undersheriff Williams from Pine

County. Your receptionist must have misunderstood when I introduced myself on the phone."

Petrich sat up. "Oh, sorry, Sheriff Williams," he said. "I just assumed that John was calling. He's the only person I know at the department, although I've heard of you. You have quite a reputation for solving some tough crimes up there, Williams."

"Thanks, Senator. As a matter-of-fact, we have another tough one. I was wondering if you could make a few minutes in your day for me. I'd like to discuss it with you."

"Discuss away. I've got a few minutes before my committee meeting."

"Actually, I think that we'd better sit down together. This is not an appropriate discussion for the phone. Do you have some time open this afternoon, or tonight? I'd be happy to drive down."

Petrich picked up a Cross pen from the top of his desk and started to drum on his daily planner. "I'm awfully busy, Williams. Could you tell me what this is about?"

"A young woman," Dan said, "disappeared from a trailer court near Sturgeon Lake last night."

"Well, I'm sorry to hear that, Sheriff. But I don't see how that would relate to me."

"You were seen at the trailer last night, Senator. We just need to get some information. Routine."

Petrich froze for a second, then quickly composed himself. He hoped the pause in the conversation hadn't said more than he wanted to reveal. "I'm sorry, Williams, but your witness must have been mistaken. I haven't been to Sturgeon Lake in years. I don't know how I could be of any help."

"It would only take a little of your time, Senator, and I'm sure that we could resolve any questions that have come up. Would two o'clock be a good time?"

"Really, Sheriff," said Petrich, in as soothing a tone as he could muster, "there must be some mistake. The old woman must have seen someone else. I haven't been to Sturgeon Lake in years. Now, I'm late to my committee meeting so I have to go. It was nice talking to you." He let the receiver drop into its cradle.

Petrich just sat there for a moment, thinking. Finally he pressed the button linking his phone to the receptionist's desk.

"Yes, Senator?"

"Laura, get Tom in here right away, please."

"But, Senator, he's meeting with the governor's aide about funding that highway project."

"Laura, honey, I don't care if he's meeting with the President of the United States. I need him in my office in five minutes, now get him in here ASAP."

"Yes, sir. I'll see what I can do."

Petrich pulled out a bundle of business cards and removed the rubber band. He quickly leafed through them, pulled out the one he was seeking and punched numbers into the phone.

"Mayor Jacobson's office, this is Mary, may I help you?"

"Hello. Please tell Mayor Jacobson that Senator Petrich is on the phone and that it's urgent."

"Of course, Senator. One moment please."

Within thirty seconds Allen Jacobson, the mayor of Pine City was on the phone. "Senator! It's a pleasure to hear from you."

"This will not be a pleasure, Al, I assure you. I just had a call from Undersheriff Williams in the sheriff's department. He wanted to drive down and talk to me about some girl who disappeared up there. He said someone saw me there. Listen, I don't have time for this tomfoolery. I'm hoping you can get Williams off my back."

"Orrin, you know I don't have that kind of pull with the sheriff's department. They're county, I'm city. I just ... "

"Goddammit, Al. You're the Democratic mayor in the biggest city in that hick county, and mostly because of me. Now, I'm telling you, I don't have time for this crap. I want you to pull every string that you can to put an end to this harassment. I want you to do it now, and I don't want my name mentioned in connection with that missing girl."

"Orrin, hold on. We don't even know what happened out there. As far as we know, the girl just up and ran off somewhere."

"I don't give a shit about the details of this whole stinking mess. I want out of the picture. Do you understand?"

"Sure," the mayor replied. "But, like I said, I'm not too sure how I can influence it."

"Listen to me, Al. Now we're going to get down to the nitty-gritty on this. You know you owe me. Besides, I'll pull every dollar of state aide from your backwater town. I'll see that the state school-aide-formula gets cut like we did to the fucking suburban districts who always vote Republican. There won't be a dollar available to fix your sewers and the Pollution Control Agency will be there to condemn them this afternoon. Do I need make myself any clearer?

"Well, Orrin, I ... I ... "

"Quit spluttering, Al. Listen! Just get him off my ass, and do it like yesterday!"

Petrich hung up, and couldn't keep from smiling, despite the seriousness of the matter.

Orrin Petrich's aide, Tom Hansen, was standing next to the receptionist when he saw the light go off on the phone console. He quickly detached himself from the pretty, young thing that he'd hired to dress up the senator's outer office and ducked into the inner sanctum.

"You wanted to see me, Senator?"

"Yes, I wanted to see you. Close that damned door."

Hansen closed the door and sat in the leather guest chair across from the senator's desk.

"I got a call from Pine County. It seems that someone said they saw me at Jeanie's trailer last night. He wanted to come down and talk to me about it." Petrich stood up and started to pace back and forth across the office. "I just called that pipsqueak mayor from Pine City and told him to call off the dogs. He tried to beg off, but I think I put the fear of God in him. We'll see if he's got the balls to bully some folks around."

"He's just city, Orrin. I don't think he'll pull much weight with the sheriff's department."

"Then that little pipsqueak will never make it beyond the mayor's job if I can help it!" exclaimed the senator. Then, somewhat more calmly, he said, "Anyway, I'm thinking the same thing. That's what I called you in here for, Tom. What else do you advise?"

"Sir, I think that you'd do better with the county attorney. He's elected, and he can pull the investigation out of the sheriff's department. Or maybe the state attorney general can claim jurisdiction because of … multiple municipalities or something. We've definitely got some players over there who can keep your name out of it."

"Well, let's leave the AG as a trump card, for now. You call the county attorney and lean on him. Just try to get this fucking thing fixed so we can get on with our business."

"I'll get to work on it, sir."

"Tom, you're a good man. I've always been able to count on you."

"Thank you, sir."

"Now, I've got some highway projects to allocate for next year."

Chapter 8

Williams rapped on the doorframe to John Sepanen's office. The sheriff looked up from a pile of vouchers.

"Come on in Dan. What's up?"

"I assume you've heard about the mess at Jean Oinen's trailer?"

The sheriff nodded. "Floyd Swenson updated me at the end of the night shift."

"I just got off the phone with Orrin Petrich."

"The senator? What's he got to do with this case?"

"We got a witness says she saw him at Oinen's trailer last night."

"I'll be damned! What did he say?"

"Not much. I wanted to talk to him face-to-face. I offered to drive to St. Paul. He wouldn't have it. Damned if I don't think he's stonewalling me."

"Well, if he's mixed up in something, you'd expect that. So, you think there's something more there?"

"Oh, I *know* there's more. I talked to the neighbors, the girl's father, and a Moose Lake elementary school teacher this morning. It seems that Jean Oinen has a little entertainment business going. The teacher named a lot of local businessmen that are regulars. He didn't know who, but he said some big name politician was a regular and that Jean Oinen didn't like him very well. The neighbor saw Orrin Petrich leaving her trailer last night. *Voila!*"

"How come we didn't know about this little prostitution business?"

"Nothing's happened to call it to our attention. We can't be in everybody's bedroom, John."

Sepanen smiled. "Petrich is a pretty heavy force in the State Senate. He plays all the political games. Obviously, he doesn't want people to know he was frequenting a prostitute. Wouldn't look so good during the next campaign." The sheriff took a match from a silver tray and lit a cigar.

Williams slid down in his chair and pulled a roll of Tums from his pocket. He pushed two off the end with his fingernail and popped them into his mouth. "There may be more to it than that. He tried to play it cool, but I can feel it."

"I know a little about Petrich. He's a big name and he's powerful." The sheriff took a deep draw on the cigar and blew the smoke toward the ceiling. "He controls a lot of money and his power would be compromised by a scandal. Don't underestimate these political cats, Dan. They carry big sticks and they're ready to use them. They want the limelight, but only above the table."

There was a knock and the sheriff's office door creaked open. Williams turned to see Mayor Allen Jacobson standing in the door. "Hi, John, Dan. Can I come in? You're the two people I need to talk to."

The sheriff looked to Williams, who shrugged. "Dan and I have talked one another out already. What's up, Al?"

The mayor shuffled in and took the other visitor's chair. He looked a decade older than his fifty years and he was stooped, like he had a constant pain in his back.

"Dan, I don't know what you said to Orrin Petrich, but you dropped a beehive into his shorts. He called me and threatened to have the EPA condemn our sewers and then cut off state funding for the repairs if I couldn't get you to stop harassing him. What did you say?"

Williams shot a quick glance at the sheriff. "I just needed his statement about a recent crime. I offered to drive down to talk, and he slammed the door on me."

"Phew, he was hot when he got hold of me," Jacobson said. "Can you help get him off my back? He's got serious clout and could do us some real damage if he stays angry." He looked pleadingly back and forth between the two men.

Sepanen smiled. "I'll call Dan off for a while, Al. If Petrich calls, tell him that it's all taken care of. If he has any questions, tell him I was very sensitive to his situation and he should feel free to call me directly. Okay?"

"Thanks, John. I appreciate it," Jacobson said, with obvious relief. He got up from the chair and headed toward the door. "I sure hope this doesn't foul up your investigation."

"Don't worry about it. And thanks for coming over, Al."

Williams shot Sepanen a look of concern, but all he saw was the smile that the mayor was getting. They sat quietly until they could hear the sound of the mayor's footsteps going down the hall.

"I can't drop Petrich from the investigation," Dan implored. "I've got an eyewitness who puts him at the scene of the crime."

"You won't drop Petrich, Dan. I assume that you've got other things to follow up on for a while?"

"I've got a list of seven or eight other customers to talk to, and a notebook with dates to find. But Petrich may have been the last person to be at the scene."

"Work around him for a while. Let things cool off. If he's involved somehow, his name will come up again and again. In the meanwhile, let me call a friend in the state patrol. He's assigned to the governor's office, maybe he can discreetly poke around St. Paul for us."

Williams shrugged. "Okay, but I'd really like to stick it to that sucker. I hate it when people try to pull shit like this. It leaves a bad taste in my mouth."

The sheriff leaned back and put his feet up on the desk. "Let me play some cards this hand, partner. This political stuff goes better with finesse than a push. We'll get the information and Petrich will never know it's happening."

"All right. This political crap is your bailiwick, anyway." Williams headed for the door, then snapped his finger, and wheeled back toward the desk. "When I was talking to Petrich and told him someone had seen him there, I didn't mention the person's sex. But he said something like 'the woman must have been mistaken.' I didn't catch it at the time but if that sucker wasn't there, how'd he know it was a woman who identified him?"

Sepanen smiled and nodded. "Lucky guess, maybe?"

Chapter 9

Under Sheriff Williams drove back to the trailer in Sturgeon Lake. Inside the trailer, the two deputies, Sandy Maki and Pam Ryan, were working overtime. Sandy Maki was taking fingerprints off all the lamps and fixtures. Dan could see Pam Ryan down the hall in the bedroom trying to get samples of the blood splatters from the carpeting.

"Well, good morning, y'all," said Williams. "I see you two are doing your usual bang-up job." He nodded to Pam.

"You know us, Dan. Just perfect, that's all," said Pam with a bright smile.

"Oh, yeah, you got that right," said Sandy. "Especially on our own time."

Dan smiled. "Own time? You should know by now we don't have time off in the Pine County sheriff's office, Sandy."

"It's beginning to sink in," Sandy said.

"Did you look at any of the dishes, Sandy?"

Sandy looked up from dusting the living room lamp. "No, there weren't any dirty ones. I figured I'd only get the resident's prints from anything in the cupboards."

"Well, I had a tip from a regular visitor to Miss Oinen's little entertainment business here that part of the routine was to tip a couple, then wash up the glasses before they'd jump in the sack."

Pam gave Dan a funny look. She had come out of the bedroom to join them. "What are you talking about? She was *entertaining* people?"

"Hey, Pam," said Sandy, grinning. "Haven't you ever *entertained* people before?"

"Not if it's what I think it is, buddy," said Pam.

"You got it," said Dan. "The occupant was a prostitute. She was apparently entertaining some very influential people, so keep your eyes open for anything that could give us names. By the way, have you seen a leather-bound notebook? I guess she kept some sort of appointment book around here someplace."

"Not out here," said Sandy. "I didn't look in the back."

"Yeah," said Pam. "Old Deputy Sandy here couldn't take the smell back there. Kept tossing his cookies until he had the dry heaves."

The young deputy's face flushed. "Dammit, Dan, you know about how I react to blood."

Williams laughed. "Yeah, I know, Sandy. I know. How about it, Pam? Did you see anything?"

"No," Pam replied, "I haven't seen anything like that."

"Let's take a look," said Williams.

They walked down the short hallway past the bloody bathroom and into the bedroom. Next to the door was the secretary desk. The door on the front was open, but there was no sign of a leather-bound planner.

"I dusted some bank records in the desk drawers. Everything on the desk is clean, so you can touch it," said Pam.

Williams stepped up to the desk, lifted the working surface exposing the single lap drawer. Inside were several neatly bound stacks of papers and bankbooks, each with a single rubber band holding it.

"Jean Oinen is pretty well off," said Pam. "Look at the passbook from the Pine Brook Bank."

Williams opened the top passbook and leafed through the pages. Each page noted regular deposits of several hundred dollars two or three times a week. The balance after the latest entry was nearly two-hundred thousand dollars. The other passbooks were much the same, but with lesser totals.

"I think that we're in the wrong profession." Dan said as he put the bankbooks back into the drawer.

"Um, Dan?" said Pam.

"What's the matter?"

"You said the owner was a prostitute. I don't think she was." Pam stated the observation with conviction.

"Did you know her?" Dan asked.

"Not at all. It's just that there are no condoms here." Pam walked over to a nightstand and pulled the drawer open. "Look. It's got a few sex toys, but not a condom anywhere." She closed the drawer and picked up a wicker wastebasket from the floor next to the nightstand. "And there isn't a condom wrapper or condom here either, just some facial tissues. I don't think a hooker would risk exposure to AIDS unless she was badly strung out on drugs. I haven't seen any drug paraphernalia either, so I doubt she was a user."

Dan leaned against the doorframe and considered Pam's observations. "Everyone I've spoken to indicated she was having sex with them for money."

"Sounds like she either had a mental problem, or was in denial," Pam said. "I've heard that a lot of prostitutes start out accepting gifts from the guys they entertain, then slowly start accepting cash when they begin to see the possibilities."

Dan picked up the bankbook and leafed through the pages. "It looks like Jean handled the evolution to accepting cash pretty well."

On the way back through the living room, Williams noted the small cedar box on a TV table next to the door. "Have you dusted this box yet, Sandy?"

"Yup. I'm done with it." Sandy turned and watched Williams open the box. Dan let out a low whistle and his gaze went quickly back to Maki.

"How much is in here?"

"About two hundred-fifty, loose cash. The envelope has three grand."

Dan reached in and picked up the envelope, noting the black fingerprint powder. The envelope was a standard #10, with security-printing on the interior to mask the contents. There were no marks on the outside except for the number 29, written in pencil, in the upper, left corner of the front. He put it back in the box and closed the cover.

"Looks like theft wasn't the motive. When you and Pam get done with the evidence, put the cash into an evidence bag and both of you sign off on the contents … just to keep everyone from asking questions about any of this stuff getting lost. Also,

check around with the rest of the neighbors. See if there's anyone else who might have seen something."

"Sure thing, Dan. Anything else we can do for you on our
time off?"

Williams smiled. "Cant think of anything right now, but I'll
let you know."

Williams walked outside and circled the trailer, looking for
openings in the trailer skirt, or obvious cubbyholes for stashing
things. On the opposite side from the entry door, he found an
access panel. Behind the panel were batts of fiberglass insulation and as he pulled them away he could see the pipes that ran
from the bathroom. He made a mental note to have a plumber
come and pull the traps to check for other evidence.

. . .

Williams drove to Sturgeon Lake and parked in front of the
general store. It was an old-time general store, selling everything from candy to used appliances. Inside, the hundred-year-
old floors creaked as he walked to the counter.

At the sound of Dan's steps, a middle-aged clerk raised up
from under the counter where he was restocking some plumbing parts.

Dan nodded to the man. "Is George around?"

"Yeah, I think he's doing payroll in the back."

Williams walked through the hallway, lit by dim incandescent
lights, to an old office. The desk was piled high with papers,
invoices, and bills. Behind the stack was a baldheaded man.

"Hi, George," Dan said. "Have you got a minute?"

George Fleming looked up from his checkbook and, recognizing Williams, stood to offer his hand. "Dan. How are you? I haven't seen you for a long time. How are things in the sheriff's office?"

"Things are fine, George, thanks. I've got some serious business. Can I close the door?"

"Sure, Dan, sit down." George gestured toward the couch to the side of his office and walked to the door and closed it himself. He then took an overstuffed chair alongside the couch. Both pieces of furniture looked like something from a St. Paul Summit Avenue mansion, circa 1930. They were covered in a well-worn brocade fabric that had obviously seen better days.

"What's the matter, Dan?"

"We had an incident down in a trailer near the lake last night. I understand that you know Jean Oinen. It happened in her trailer."

George grimaced. "Something happened to Jeanie?"

"We're not sure. Right now, she just seems to be missing."

"What's that got to do with me?" Fleming asked.

"I know about Jeanie's business, George. I understand you were a regular visitor."

Fleming cast a glance at the door, checking to see if anyone was near. Lowering his voice, he said,"My God, Dan. If this gets around, there are going to be lots of embarrassed folks. Um, I don't know what to say. I guess I was a *friend* of Jean's. But *customer* is a pretty strong word."

"I'm trying to put a list together of the clientele. Once we know who came and went, we can narrow down the list of people to talk to. Who else visits Jean's trailer?"

"I can't tell you that, Dan. We're talking good people, with families. I can't be the one to spill that. Besides, the ones I know would never do anything to harm a fly. Most of them are in church every Sunday."

"Don't I remember some commandment about adultery?" Dan asked.

George wiped his hand over his face. "The pastor says that God forgives those who ask forgiveness."

"Then what's the problem?"

"I don't think our wives would be quite so generous," George replied.

"You might be surprised, George. It'll go better for you as well as the others to come clean on what you know."

"Maybe not," said George. "There's more to this than you can imagine. But maybe you're right. I need to get some things off my chest."

Dan didn't reply and after a few moments the store owner shook his head. "All right, I know this is for the best, but I'll get skinned alive if these guys ever find out it was me who gave out their names." He counted nine names off on his fingers. Dan had four from previous discussions, but added the five new names to the list of clients.

"I imagine someone has already told you about the clap," George said.

"No," said Dan, feigning ignorance. "What about it?"

"Someone brought a dose into the group and it spread around to nearly everyone. I got a call from one of the guys and some-one worked out a deal with a doctor in Fond du Lac, west of Cloquet, to have us all treated discreetly. He might be able to give you a list of all the people who were treated."

"What was the doctor's name?" Dan asked.

"The same as canned salmon," George replied. "Rubenstein."

Williams left the store with five more names as well as the name of the doctor. He called information from his cell phone and was connected with Rubenstein's office, where he was surprised to be able to schedule an open appointment for that afternoon. He drove toward Fond du Lac, in Carlton County. He'd made the appointment with Dr.. Rubenstein about a case of gonorrhea. But, Rubenstein didn't know it wasn't Dan who was the one who had the problem.

. . .

Williams walked into Rubenstein's waiting room and was surprised at the number of empty chairs lining the walls. Rubenstein's office was a stark contrast to the Pine City doctor's office. Dan couldn't remember ever going to the Pine City clinic that it was not busy, most days, even long after official hours ended.

Dan walked to the receptionist's counter, but no one was around. "Anybody home?" He heard a rustle from the back and an older Native American woman, in a white dress, with many years on her face, peeked around the corner. A nameplate said, "Kay RN."

"You must be Mr. Williams." It came out half statement, half question.

"Yeah. I had a four-fifteen appointment to see the doctor."

The woman came out of the little room that she'd been working in, went behind the receptionist's counter, and looked at the appointment book.

"You bring a specimen?" She asked.

"No. I'm not sick. I need to talk to the doctor about one of his patients." Dan pulled his badge holder from the pocket of his jacket and showed it to the woman. She looked at him curiously only for a moment.

"All right, Officer. Just follow me, please."

Dan began to follow her down the hall, when she paused. "Just a moment, Officer Williams," she said. She went into the room where she'd been working, pulled a stool up to a microscope and started to click a counter as she stared into the eyepieces. When she finished she made a note on a chart and looked up at Williams who was leaning on the doorframe.

"The doctor is waiting for this," she explained. She stood up and walked passed Williams. She rapped once on the door to another room. Dan heard a muffled response. The nurse peeked around the door and passed the chart through. Williams could hear some mumbled words, then she came back.

"We'll put you in room one," said the nurse, as she led him down the hall. "Dr. Rubenstein is almost done. There are some magazines in there if you want to read while you're waiting."

Williams was reading a two-year-old *Field & Stream* when Dr. Rubenstein walked into the room. Dan rose and introduced himself. Dan towered over the smaller man. He was nearly a foot shorter than Dan and had a slender build. His hair was dark and he looked like his heritage might be Mediterranean.

"Dr. Rubenstein, I'm investigating a missing-person case in Sturgeon Lake, a young woman, and I was advised that she is one of your patients—Jean Oinen?"

The doctor sat down on a stool at the small desk and rubbed his eyes. He looked tired. "I can't say that name sounds familiar, Sheriff. I'm sorry, I can't remember anything about her right offhand."

"Dr. Rubenstein, I've just been informed that you were the physician who treated cases of clap among her customers. Does the name sound familiar now?"

"I'm afraid you're mistaken. I've never treated more than a rare case of gonorrhea. Could you be speaking to the wrong doctor? I don't usually have patients from that far away."

"Doctor, with all due respect, I know that Jean, and a number of her close personal friends, were sharing a social disease. More than one of them said they'd been to you for treatment. Now, I suppose we could pull the Department of Health in on this because the law says you have to report all cases of gonorrhea to them."

Dan had the doctor's full attention now. "Um, well, now that I think about it, I seem to recall there was an incident, but it seems to me it was chlamydia, not gonorrhea. Chlamydia infections are not reported to anyone. Beyond that, I have to state that I cannot reveal private information about my patients to you without a court order."

"Jean Oinen is missing," Dan said. "The inside of her trailer is covered in blood. The medical examiner says whoever lost the blood is probably dead. At this point, we're assuming Jean Oinen is the victim of a vicious attack. The more I know about Jean and her customers, the better my chances are of tracking down her attacker."

Rubenstein's tired face went serious. "Well, of course, that's terrible to hear. Still, Sheriff, I'm sorry, but without specific evidence of Jean's death, my hands are tied."

"Well," Dan offered, "let's talk in generalities. Can you tell me roughly how many people you treated?"

Rubenstein considered the situation and replied, "Roughly, twenty or twenty-five."

"All men, from the Sturgeon Lake area?"

"They weren't all men. I also treated some women who had been intimate with the men involved. And the geography was wider than Sturgeon Lake."

"Did you treat wives?" Dan asked.

"One or two, as I remember."

"Would one of the male patients happen to be a political figure?"

Rubenstein closed his eyes and pinched the bridge of his nose. "I really can't get into that. Is that kind of thing pertinent to your investigation?"

"I believe there has been a serious assault on a young woman by one or more of her customers. Like I said, the more I can find out about those customers, the more I can rule out suspects. We know that Orrin Petrich was at her trailer shortly before she disappeared."

"Hmmm. I don't think that I can help you any further without a court order," said the doctor, rising abruptly. "Now, if you'll excuse me, I have patients to attend to."

Not Many, Dan thought. He persisted. "If I gave you a list of names, would you confirm or deny that they were treated by you?"

"I think that would violate physician-patient privilege. Really, Sheriff Williams … "

"Two more questions," Dan said, ignoring the obvious attempts at dismissal. "What did you prescribe to treat these people?"

"As I recall, plain old penicillin. Your other question?"

"Were you one of the customers, too?" Dan asked.

"Mr. Williams, my private life is certainly none of your business. As I said, I have patients to attend to." The doctor turned and walked out of the room and into a door halfway down the hallway, closing the door behind him.

Williams walked out and was about to leave the waiting room when he turned to the nurse, still sitting behind the desk. He could see she was working on a crossword puzzle.

"Nurse, what does the doctor prescribe to treat chlamydia?"

"It varies. He's the expert on that."

"How about gonorrhea?"

A smile broke out on her face and she made a mock injection from a large imaginary syringe. "A big dose of penicillin, in the butt. Hurts like hell. I think it's divine justice, personally."

"You ever give one of those to a political big shot?" Dan asked. "Like maybe Orrin Petrich?"

Her smile grew even wider. "Sorry, Deputy, I couldn't tell you something like that."

"No harm in trying," said Dan with a grin. He turned and started out of the room.

"Deputy?" Williams turned back. "He called me a bitch when I stuck him." She winked. "And his name doesn't show up in any file."

. . .

Dan pulled into his home driveway. It had been fourteen hours since he'd left. The lights were on in the kitchen and his stomach reminded him that it was suppertime, although his head felt it should be bedtime.

Inside, Sally was stuffing a casserole into the microwave oven. She had changed from the clinic's uniform of flowered surgical scrubs to a maroon, University of Minnesota sweatshirt, and a pair of jeans. She pecked his cheek as Dan slipped off his buckskin jacket. On the table was a half-finished plate of some sort of hot dish. He headed right to the refrigerator and pulled out a bottle of Michelob draft beer.

"Long day," Sally said. "Are you in for the evening now?"

He plopped in the other kitchen chair as the microwave buzzer announced that his dinner was warm. "I hope so. It's been a hell of a day."

"What was the call this morning?"

"Crazy deal," Dan replied. "Probably a murder, but no body. The missing girl was apparently a prostitute working out of a trailer down by Sturgeon Lake. Neighbors heard a scream, but didn't see anyone. Later they heard the door slam and found blood."

Sally carried the casserole over to the table and scooped three big ladles of the meat and vegetable mixture onto the plate. "So you don't know if she's dead?"

"Tony Oresek says there was enough loss of blood to kill someone; but no, we're not sure yet."

"Any suspects?"

"Half the men in Sturgeon Lake, Moose Lake and Willow River. The neighbors in the trailer park saw two of them coming or going last night."

Sally shuddered slightly as she considered Dan's comments. "I hate the thought of creeps like that living around here. I hear about the prostitution sweeps the cops make in St. Paul and wonder what kind of person would pay for sex."

"Creeps," Dan said. "Half of them are politicians and the other half are local businessmen." He ate as he waited for her reaction.

Sally stared at him. "Are you serious? Politicians and businessmen?"

"If I told you who, you'd be shocked."

She leaned forward on her hands as if waiting for him to start listing them.

"Sorry. This is a little too sensitive for the rumor mongers. I *can* tell you that one state senator has already been twisting arms to get his name off the list."

"Oh, really?" she said sarcastically. "You think he believes it might make his reelection bid a little tougher?"

"There may be more to it than that. He wouldn't even talk to me about it. He's trying to stonewall. He sicked the Pine City mayor on Sepanen. Sepanen played a delaying game and he's following up on Petrich discreetly. I'm chasing down some of the others."

"How'd they keep something like this quiet in a little town?" Sally asked. "Everyone knows what everyone else is doing. I know where the Heffernan boy went on his last date, what he was wearing, and that he got to second base."

"Apparently there is a good-old-boys' network going on here. They only got in through referrals, so everyone was at risk through any weak link."

"They were all lucky she never got pregnant or anything. What a stink!"

"Someone brought in a case of chlamydia, or gonorrhea, or something, and passed it around so that they all had to get a penicillin shot. Even a couple of wives were in on that. I would have loved to hear those explanations!"

"They don't treat chlamydia with penicillin, Dan," Sally said. "I transcribe the doctor's notes and they treat chlamydia with tetracycline. What made you say penicillin?"

"The doctor who treated them told me he gave them all penicillin shots to cure their chlamydia."

"Well, Dear, he's either lying or a quack."

. . .

At 6:55 p.m. Ann Olsen dialed Jean Oinen's phone and waited for an answer. After five rings she hung up. She dialed again at 7:55, 8:55 and 9:55 p.m., hoping she could catch Jean at the top of the hour between visitors. There never was an answer.

Chapter 10

The operator pushed the flashing button on the console. "Pine County emergency services. How can I help you?" The CRT screen display for the enhanced 911 system indicated that the call was from rural Duquette. A fire-number address, 1437, on County Road 11, and a phone number followed the name, "Eric Olsen." The voice was so faint that the dispatcher couldn't make out what the woman was saying. "I'm sorry, ma'am. I can't hear you. Is this a medical emergency?" The voice came back a little stronger.

"This is Ann Olsen. There's someone downstairs. A burglar, I think."

The operator dialed the number to transfer the call to the Pine County sheriff's department dispatcher. "I've got the Pine County sheriff's dispatcher on the line, Mrs. Olsen. Go ahead."

"There's someone downstairs," Ann Olsen said, her voice quavering. "I can hear them walking around and opening doors. Please send someone quick!" There was panic in her voice, now, but it was still little more than a whisper.

"I hear you, ma'am. Hold for one second while I dispatch a

deputy to assist you."

The sheriff's dispatcher pushed the button on the console that activated her headset. "Any available deputy, please respond."

"I'm contacting our squad," the dispatcher said to Ann Olsen. "I'll have someone on the way in a minute. Hang on."

"Dispatch, I'm clear." Pam Ryan's voice responded.

"I've got a burglary in progress on County 11, fire-number 1437, north of Duquette. What's your ETA?"

"I'm west of Sturgeon Lake, at least twelve minutes away. I'm coming, but can you see if the highway patrol or Moose Lake has someone closer?" The dispatcher rolled her eyes and thought she was glad it wasn't her in the Olsen house with an intruder.

"Ten-four." She switched back from the radio to the phone. "Ma'am, the deputy is coming, but it's going to take a few minutes. Can you get out of the house?"

"I ... I don't think so. I'd have to get the baby." Suddenly the voice started to rise. "He's coming up the stairs. Hurry!" Then the line went dead.

The dispatcher quickly switched the radio to the state patrol frequency. There was no state squad closer than Carlton—at least twenty-five minutes away.

She switched frequencies again. "Moose Lake PD. This is Pine County dispatch."

"Go, Pine County."

"I have a burglary in progress on County 11, fire-number 1437, north of Duquette. I have a deputy enroute, but she's ten-minutes out. Can you respond?"

"I'm on my way. ETA, five minutes."

"Thanks, Moose Lake. I have a Mrs. Olsen in the house with a baby."

The dispatcher went back to the Pine County frequency. "Deputy Ryan, I have Moose Lake PD with an ETA of five minutes. You'll be backing them up."

. . .

Ann Olsen hung up the phone and grabbed the old, single-shot shotgun from the bedroom closet. She'd seen Eric load it a few times. As she fumbled for the box of shells, they fell from the shelf and scattered over the floor with a crash. She stepped on one and cried out in pain.

Ann looked around the moonlit room to make sure that the intruder wasn't there. Groping on the floor in the dark shadows she picked up one shell, then pulled the hammer back. The breach didn't open. She located the lever that released the breach and felt the forearm fall toward the floor as she pushed the lever to the side. She set the shell into the open barrel and listened to it fall into place with a dull clunk. As her heart raced as she struggled to close the breach. On the third try, the barrel clicked shut. Her hands shook as she knelt in the doorway and she could barely hold the gun steady. She peeked around the doorjamb and down the darkened hallway. She couldn't make out anyone. She climbed to her feet and scampered across the hallway to the baby's room.

The door slammed behind her as she ran to the crib and swept the baby into one arm while she supported the shotgun in the other. Suddenly, light swept under the door as someone turned on the hallway light. The old floor creaked as feet made their way to the door, and then past. Ann's heart pounded and she barely dared take a breath.

The footsteps stopped, then approached the room again. She tried to call out a threat to shoot, but her vocal cords were frozen in fear. She watched in terror as the doorknob turned. Ann lifted the shotgun with one hand.

BOOM! The deafening explosion and flash of the shotgun's discharge blinded her, threw her backward, and her ears went numb. Somewhere, in the darkness, a phone was ringing.

. . .

Officer Mike Ronning glanced at the clock on the dash. It was 11:37 p.m. as he crossed the freeway bridge on County Line Road. "Five minutes is a long time to wait when you've got a burglar in the house," he said to himself. Luckily, he thought, most burglars just wanted to grab something of value and make a run. They weren't interested in hurting anyone. They often made a quick exit unless cornered.

As he raced through the night a deer's eyes appeared on the right edge of the road. "Stay put, baby." He eased the squad to the left edge of the road and maintained his 105 miles per hour. The deer didn't move, apparently transfixed by the flashing lights. As he passed, it bounded away from him.

THUD!

"Shit!" Ronning wrestled the steering wheel to stay on the road as the impact of a second deer coming from the shadows hit the driver's side fender. A flash of brown went past his window, ripping off the spotlight and side mirror with a crash. He maintained control of the squad, and continued on, minus the left set of headlights.

"Lord, I hope that we didn't poke a hole in the radiator," Ronning mumbled. A quick glance showed the temperature gauge was steady.

The Pine City dispatcher dialed the number in Duquette, but there was no answer. She let it ring in the hope that if she couldn't raise any of the Olsens, it might scare the burglar. The clock showed 11:40 p.m. One more minute, or so, before the first squad would arrive.

At County Road 11, Ronning turned south, and met an old, red pickup. He watched the fire numbers. The rural homes didn't have addresses, just a fire number. The number got closer to 1400. Finally, he saw the sign, 1429. He eased off the accelerator and announced, "Pine County. Moose Lake is at the scene."

As 1433 passed he turned off the light bar and siren. "How far out is your deputy?" Ronning asked the dispatcher.

"Still five minutes plus."

Ronning pulled in the driveway at number 1437. The house was not visible through the trees. He rolled down the driveway and an old farmhouse came into view. Lights were on in two of the upstairs rooms.

"Pine County, I have lights on in two rooms. There is no sign of activity, no vehicles in sight." The clock on the dash showed 11:43 p.m.

Ronning parked the car with the headlights shining on the front door. It appeared to be open a crack. His heart was pounding. He didn't feel right about entering the house without back-up, but with a lone woman and baby inside, he felt compelled to move quickly.

He pulled his Smith & Wesson 9mm automatic from its holster as he ran to the side of the front door. He eased over to a window and stole a quick peek inside. The room appeared to be a living room. It was dark and there was no sign of any person.

From somewhere in the distance, he heard the sound of an engine starting. He listened, but it sounded like it might have been at the next house, maybe an eighth of a mile away. He could hear the wail of a siren, still far in the distance, sound carrying well in the crisp spring stillness.

Ronning eased to the door with his back to the frame. Inside he could hear the incessant ringing of the phone. He looked through the crack of the open door but saw nothing.

Bang! The door flew back against the wall as Ronning kicked it open and ran into the room in a shooter's crouch. The flashlight, held high over his head, moved back and forth, but the beam illuminated only furniture. Between rings of the phone, he could hear the muffled crying of a baby somewhere upstairs.

"Mrs. Olsen. Are you here? This is the Moose Lake police."

There was no reply. He moved quickly from room to room; dining room, big enough for a large farm family; large kitchen; pantry, stocked with home-canned vegetables. The back door, an exit from the kitchen, was open.

Ronning was starting up the stairs when the approaching siren stopped. The upstair's hallway light was on. At the top of the stairs, Ronning quickly looked in both directions. No one was in sight, but the floor to the right was littered with wood chips.

He moved down the hallway to the right, toward the sound of

the crying. At the first door, he stopped. There was a splintered hole in the old pine door, slightly larger than a softball, just above the doorknob. He pushed the door open with his left hand and leaned back. The lights were on, but there was no sound from inside except the crying of a baby. He peeked around the doorframe and his heart stopped. The room smelled of the nitrates from burnt gunpowder. On the floor was a chunky, blonde woman with a pool of blood around her head. From somewhere under her robe came the cries of a baby. Next to her on the floor, lay an old, single-shot shotgun. Ronning moved to her side and knelt, feeling for a pulse in her neck. It was strong, but rapid.

"Moose Lake?" The call came from downstairs.

"Upstairs. Call for an ambulance. I've got a woman down, with a head wound."

Ronning opened the woman's robe, exposing a very small baby tucked against her bare abdomen. The white, flannel nightgown was crumpled above the woman's waist. The baby's legs were under the woman's torso. He rolled the woman back a little and pulled the baby out, snuggling it up against his chest. "Okay, little baby. Shhhh. It's okay. It's okay"

He bounced the baby gently, talking softly as he scanned the scene. The shotgun caught his eye. The barrel looked slightly bent and there were a few blonde hairs stuck to the barrel.

Pine County Deputy Pam Ryan showed up at the door with her pistol in one hand and a first-aid kit in the other.

"What have we got?" She looked at the woman on the floor. "Is she alive?" Ryan holstered her weapon and knelt down beside the woman. She opened the first-aid kit and pulled out a pair of latex gloves.

"So far," Ronning replied. "Not much bleeding now. Steady breathing. Nasty gash on the head. I'll bet she's got a concussion, or fractured skull."

"The Duquette first responders are on the way, and so is the ambulance from Mercy Hospital." Ryan opened a gauze pad and pressed it against the gash on Ann Olsen's head. When she removed the pad, she noticed that very little blood flowed back into the gash. She looked at the nightgown, rumpled and pulled up high on Olsen's breast and wondered if the attack had involved sexual assault. "How's the baby?"

Ronning held the baby out for inspection and surveyed for damage. There was a nasty bruise on one side of the head, and one of the legs was twisted at an odd angle. "He's got a nasty rap on the head. Looks like he's got a broken leg, too. Probably from when mama fell down on top of him. I had to take her off the poor tyke."

The baby had been crying continuously throughout this exchange.

"Did you check the rest of the house?" Ryan asked.

"The downstairs. I didn't get any further than this, up here. I assume that whoever was here, is gone. I heard an engine start next door, when I was coming in."

Ryan stood up, then disappeared down the hall with her gun drawn. She came back in less than a minute. "Mom's room is over there." She nodded toward the room across the hall. "There's a box of shotgun shells scattered on the floor. The other room is empty, and so is the bathroom."

The sound of crunching gravel came from the driveway.

"First responders. I'll show them up." Ryan disappeared.

Ronning looked down at Ann Olsen again. She continued to breathe regularly and deeply.

Pam Ryan led two young men into the bedroom. Ronning continued to hold the crying baby. He looked helplessly at Pam. "Would you mind taking the kid? I'm not much good with'em."

Pam, who was unmarried and childless, looked pathetically at Ronning. "OK, Ronning, but let's make it clear ... it's not my role as the female on the scene to be the designated baby-sitter." Ronning blushed but gave the child up gratefully. Pam began to coo and rock the baby gently. The crying stopped. The two male firemen smiled knowingly at one another.

Ronning knelt down and examined the shotgun on the floor. "Look at the bend in the barrel," Ronning pointed out to Pam. "And it looks like there's some blood and a couple blonde hairs are stuck in the bend."

"That's what he hit her with," Pam said. The baby began to cry again

Ronning walked to the hallway, Pam following, as the fireman put sterile gauze pads on Ann Olsen's head. Ronning ran his hand over the plaster wall opposite the room.

"Looks like the wall caught the pellets. I don't see any blood. Looks like that woman took a shot through the door and missed. He must have grabbed the gun, then walloped her over the head with the barrel. Probably grabbed something and ran."

"Or, got scared and ran without anything," Pam speculated, still rocking the baby gently. In the distance, another siren wailed.

"I'll bet that's our ambulance." Pam Ryan, said, and walked

down the stairs with the crying child.

. . .

Pam walked around the yard with the baby while Ronning brought the ambulance crew in the house. Behind the house there were some faint footprints in the frosty grass, leading away from the back door. They cut across the lawn, going south, and disappeared into the grove of balsam fir trees. She decided not to follow them through the thick tree branches with the baby in her arms.

"Well, junior. I think this is as far as you and I go," Pam said to the infant.

There was the sound of another approaching siren and Pam walked back to the front yard in time to see a second Pine County squad pull into the driveway. She recognized Tom Thompson, a Pine County sergeant.

"Hey, Ryan, what are you doing here? Day care?"

Pam gave him a look of disgust. "The baby is injured. I'm holding him until the ambulance crew gets through with the mother. What took you so long to get here?"

"I was in the southwest corner of the county when the call came through."

"You sure that's your excuse, Sergeant?" She pointed to white powder on Thompson's uniform shirt. "You sure you weren't eating powdered-sugar doughnuts and drinking coffee?"

Thompson smiled. He liked the plucky new deputy and their joking relationship. "Where's the Moose Lake cop?"

"He's inside with the ambulance crew." Pam nodded toward

the front door.

"What have we got inside?" Thompson asked.

"Woman on the floor with a head wound," Pam replied. "Looks like she fired a shotgun at the intruder, but missed. The blast blew a hole through the door upstairs. The burglar probably whacked her over the head with the barrel of the gun. We left the shotgun on the floor until we take some crime-scene photos." She paused, then added, "the mother's nightgown was pushed up, around her waist. She may have been sexually assaulted, too."

"Any sign of the intruder?"

"Nothing. The Moose Lake cop heard a car start to the south when he was about to enter the house. There are footprints out the back door going toward the neighbor's house."

Ronning walked out the front door with Pam Ryan's first-aid kit. "She's starting to come around. She started to moan. Still not coherent yet, but the ambulance crew said she'll be okay. Her pupils have uneven dilation—probably a concussion."

"Anything missing inside?" Thompson asked.

"Not that I can see. There's an older television, a new microwave, no VCR; but I can't see any connections for it either. The master bedroom is undisturbed. Maybe my siren scared them off."

The baby continued to cry. "Does he need a diaper changed?" Thompson asked Pam Ryan.

She sniffed at the top of the diaper. "Doesn't smell like it." She ran her free hand over the baby's head and torso. The crying intensified when she touched the leg. "There's a pretty big knot on his head, and his foot is at a funny angle.I think he has a broken leg, too."

"You think it's a boy?" Ronning asked.

Pam rolled her eyes. "He's dressed in blue pajamas. Unless they're hand-me-downs, I'd guess the baby is a he."

"I think I'll follow the footprints and see where they end," Ronning said. He started across the lawn with the beam of his flashlight following the footprints in the frosty grass.

The entourage of first responders and the Moose Lake ambulance crew came through the front door carrying the stretcher. There was a nondescript lump, covered with blankets strapped to it. The deputies watched the crew lift the stretcher into the back of the ambulance, then walked over to the rear ambulance doors as the first responders left.

"Hey, boys," Pam called out. "You'd better take junior along, too. He's got a nasty bruise on his head, and his left leg is twisted. He was trapped under his mom when she fell down."

One of the EMT's finished latching the gurney into place and reached out to take the baby. "We'll take care of him."

"His mom will probably get real excited if she comes around and he's not around," said Pam.

Thompson closed the rear ambulance door and watched as they backed onto the road and drove off.

Ronning came up from behind them. "There's fresh tire tracks in the driveway next door. Nobody home. The footprints lead right up to the tire tracks. The frost helps a lot."

"Pam, I heard the engine start before you got here. Did you meet anyone on the road?"

"No. Nothing since I crossed the freeway. It either went north or waited until I passed before pulling out."

Thompson looked at the lights blazing in the house. "Thanks for the help, Mike. You might have saved that woman's life by showing up when you did. FAX down a copy of your report when you get it written up. Pam, check around for any more evidence and see if you can get hold of a husband or relative. I'm going to take a run to Mercy Hospital and see if I can talk to the woman when she comes around."

As Thompson left, he heard Pam say, "Hey, Ronning, what happened to the front of your squad?"

. . .

Sergeant Tom Thompson sat alone in the emergency-room waiting area, reading magazines and listening to the infrequent calls on his lapel-mounted radio. It had been a quiet weeknight, even in the emergency room, until Ann Olsen had been attacked.

The clock said 3:33 a.m. when the doctor, in green surgical scrubs, walked into the waiting area. "Officer, the boy is okay. Got a broken leg and a few bruises, but that seems to be all. Mrs. Olsen is drifting in and out of consciousness. I'm afraid she can't talk to you. She asked for her husband once and then slipped away."

"How serious are her injuries?"

"Fractured skull. That's about it, except for this." He pulled a small Zip-Lock plastic bag from the back pocket of the surgical scrub pants. Inside was some moist, white material that looked like partially dissolved aspirin. He gave the bag to Thompson.

"What is it?" Thompson held the bag up to the light.

"I don't know. I was having a devil of a time trying to get her stabilized. The symptoms didn't fit with the head injury. I was looking for signs of rape and noticed a little white residue on one buttock. Her rectum was full of it. I saved this for evidence, but I irrigated the rest."

"What do you think was going on?"

"I thought it was some narcotic, but the symptoms aren't right."

Thompson was lost. "It wasn't a narcotic, then?" He asked.

"Like I said, the symptoms aren't right."

"So you're saying someone tried to kill her? I mean beyond the blow to the head?"

The doctor walked to one of the chairs and sat down wearily with a thud. "I'd say so. We'll know better when we find out what that stuff is, but the whole thing looks suspicious. Placing a substance like that in the rectum is a very effective way of killing a person without leaving any evidence of how it was done. The rectum is like a hypersensitive transdermal receptor. The rectal mucosae absorb small molecules rapidly, especially in liquid form, and the absorption leaves no surface indication of how a substance gets into the body. Without the knowledge that the patient had absorbed something in this way, more than likely any medical personnel would simply watch helplessly as the patient's condition deteriorates. A lot of times, it's not caught even in an autopsy, especially if there are other traumas to attribute death to."

"If the stuff absorbs rapidly, why was there still some in the rectum?" Thompson asked.

"The powder was inserted without an accompanying liquid,"

said the doctor. "Without liquid, the substance would be absorbed more slowly."

"Is she stable now?" Thompson asked.

"More or less," the doctor replied. "Her heart rate and blood pressure were dropping slowly but they're leveling out, now. I gave her a stimulant to counteract the effects of the rectal drugs, but I don't know how much of this substance she absorbed."

"If you had to make a guess, what would you tell the lab people to look for?"

"Some depressant." The doctor hesitated, then added, "One strange thing—there was no sign of any gel capsules with the powder. Whoever did this had access to bulk drugs or took the time to empty a bunch of capsules. I'd guess it might be a drug dealer."

Thompson contemplated what the doctor had just said. "Um. Whoever attacked Mrs. Olsen probably wanted it to look like a botched burglary, rather than a deliberate murder attempt," he said, more or less to himself.

Chapter 11

Williams had three notes on his desk when he arrived at his office at 8:00 a.m., one from the sheriff, one from Sergeant Tom Thompson, and one from Tony Oresek, the county medical examiner. He walked down the hallway to the sheriff's office and knocked on the frame of the open door.

"Come in, Dan, and close the door."

"What's up?" Dan asked. "You don't usually ask me to close the door."

"I want to bring you up-to-date on our friend at the capitol and I'd just as soon others don't hear it."

Dan took one of the guest chairs.

"I talked to some people in security in the state capitol. Orrin Petrich is a royal pain in the ass for everyone. He's number three in the Democratic Party's hierarchy and he likes to let everyone know about it. He never drives himself anywhere, says it wastes his productive time. His aide … " Sepanen dug through some papers on his desk, then pulled out a scrap of paper " … Tom Hansen, drives him everywhere while the esteemed state senator handles business on his cellular phone."

Sepanen stopped to let Williams digest the information. Dan nodded. "Uh huh. Go on."

"To top it all off, Petrich is the chairman of some senate committee. He deals out projects and money to his cronies and people who can buy him influence. If you are a Republican, or if you can't give him something in return, you're just shit in his eyes."

"So why is he so upset about this deal ... aside from the fact that it might soil his reputation?"

"My sources tell me he's worked hard to cultivate an image of himself as a family man. His district is rural, and the folks there are good family folks. Now, my sources say there are rumors around the capitol he isn't even living with his wife anymore. Petrich is in a situation where if all this stuff slips out, he could lose the next election."

"*Is* he living with his wife?" Dan asked.

"Apparently she maintains the house back home. He stays in an apartment in St. Paul during committee meetings and legislative sessions. I'm told the reality is that he hasn't been back to the house in a long time. Too busy."

"I still can't see what all the concern is about," Dan said. "If he's innocent, we could have a discreet little meeting and he could say she was fine when he left. End of discussion. Instead, he's pulling strings to keep me out and pretending that he was never there. I smell something rotten."

The sheriff shrugged. "The political arena is different from real life. There's no such thing as a discreet meeting in the capitol. There are eyes and ears everywhere."

"John, I've got a sixth sense in these things. There are some bones in a closet here somewhere. I want to dig them out."

"Well, of course I'll never keep you from doing that, Dan. I'm as concerned about elections as any public official, but I also have a sworn responsibility to the people of Pine County to investigate every crime to the fullest extent possible. All I want you to do is just investigate this thing with Petrich discreetly until you have something concrete. Then, let's talk. I'd like to use the back door rather than using a battering ram on the front door; at least this time. Okay?"

Dan rose from the chair. "Okay, John. We'll try to keep it as discreet as possible, but if it's like you say it is at the capitol, that's gonna make the job a lot harder."

"I know, I know," said Sepanen. "Just bear with me on this for a while, Dan."

. . .

Sergeant Tom Thompson was still sitting in the Mercy Hospital waiting room when he saw a disoriented-looking young man walk past to the nurses station. Eric Olsen looked around for a moment. Finding no one, he turned and walked to the waiting room where he had seen Sergeant Thompson.

"Excuse me, Officer; Deputy Ryan told me my wife and son are here somewhere. Can you tell me how to get hold of the nurse or doctor?"

Thompson stood up and walked over to the young man. Olsen was close to thirty, but his slender build and blonde hair made him look twenty.

"You must be Eric Olsen?"

"Yes, I'm Eric."

" I'm Sergeant Thompson. Your wife and son are doing fine, Mr. Olsen. The doctor says Mrs. Olsen is responding to the treatment. Your son has a broken leg and a big bruise, but he's doing good, too."

Olsen relaxed visibly.

"The nurse isn't here right now," Thompson said. "She'll probably be back in a few minutes. In the meantime, maybe you could answer a few questions, if that's okay?"

"You're certain they're alright?"

"I saw the doctor a few minutes ago, Mr. Olsen. Your wife and son are doing fine. The nurse should be back any moment."

Olsen, still obviously discomfited, nevertheless walked with Thompson to two chairs near the entrance of the room and sat down.

"You were away from home last night when this happened?" asked Thompson.

"Yeah. I work nights over in Askov. I don't get off work 'til seven."

"I see. Do you know any reason someone would want to hurt your wife?" asked Thompson.

"*Want* to hurt her? I'm not sure what you mean, Officer. I thought this was a burglary. Do you mean someone was *trying* to hurt her?"

"We're not absolutely sure, Mr. Olsen. Now, like I say, your wife and son are doing fine, but we suspect this could have been a deliberate attack. We think the attacker was scared off by the Moose Lake police—but there was more." Thompson shifted in his chair. His next question was going to be uncomfortable.

"Mr. Olsen, does your wife use drugs of any kind?

Olsen's look was incredulous. "Ann doesn't believe in taking medicine. She doesn't even use aspirin!"

"Well, then, it looks like the attacker tried to drug Mrs. Olsen. Whoever it was, they tried to do it in a way that was hard to detect. If the emergency room doctor hadn't been really sharp, he would have missed it and she might have died."

Olsen just shook his head in disbelief. "My God," he said, "I can't imagine anyone wanting to hurt Ann. She's about as harmless as anyone can be."

The emergency-room nurse, a matronly, competent looking woman, had apparently heard the men's voices and had returned to her desk. Eric turned and approached her, followed by Thompson.

"Are you Eric Olsen?", asked the nurse.

"Yes. Can I see Ann? Do you have some news?"

"I'll let the doctor know that you're here, Mr. Olsen. Just a moment, please."

It wasn't long before the doctor, still in his green scrubs, emerged from a curtained off area and approached them. "Mr. Olsen?"

"Yes. Are they okay? Can I see them?"

The doctor took Olsen by the elbow and led him to the chairs in the waiting room. He motioned for Thompson to follow.

"Your wife is starting to stabilize," the doctor said reassuringly. "She has a skull fracture, but she'll recover from that. She also had a big dose of something that had her blood pressure all screwed up. It's under control now, though. We're keeping a close watch on her. They're both out, right now, so neither will even know you're here. We've moved them out of emergency to another room."

"I'd just like to see them, anyway, if that's okay," insisted Olsen.

"Alright. You can go back for a while. The nurse will show you to the room.

Ted Olsen nodded affirmatively, then followed the nurse down another corridor.

The doctor turned to Thompson. "I've been doing some more thinking," he said, "and I wonder if she didn't get some barbiturates or beta-blockers. Either one would cause the symptoms I'm seeing."

Thompson shook his head. "You got me, doctor. She doesn't even use aspirin, according to her husband."

"Well, I can verify that she didn't take them herself," the doctor said. "The question is why someone would want to do that unless ... "

"You got it, Doctor" said Thompson, "My opinion is that the guy didn't want to just drug her. He wanted her dead."

. . .

Williams, back in his office, punched the numbers for the medical examiner's office in Duluth. The assistant, Eddie Paulson, answered the phone.

"Tony's not in yet, we had to pick up a body last night at a house fire and we got in pretty late."

"He left a phone message yesterday. Any idea why?" Dan asked.

"Ah, let's see. Oh, yes. We checked the blood from the trailer. It's human, type B-positive, with Kell antibodies."

Dan noted the information, then asked, "That type of blood is pretty rare, isn't it?"

"Yes. B-positive is fairly unusual," Eddie said. "Only about fourteen percent of the population has that type. The Kell antibodies are quite rare. If your missing woman had that blood type, you could be reasonably sure that it was her."

"Can I get that from her doctor?"

"Maybe. But it's not something a family practitioner would check routinely. You'd have better luck with a blood bank, or the hospital where she'd had the transfusion."

"Transfusion?" Dan asked. "What makes you think she's had a transfusion?"

"Kell antibodies are unusual. They're the result, ordinarily, of a transfusion."

"Okay, Eddie. Thanks. I'll follow up on it."

. . .

Williams sat back in the chair and reached into his pocket for the roll of Tums. He broke one off and popped it into his mouth while he thought. He reached for the phone and dialed the number of his former partner, Laurie Lone Eagle, at the Minnesota Bureau of Criminal Apprehension, in St. Paul. She picked up the phone on the first ring.

"Laurie, Dan Williams here. I was hoping that you'd be able to help me out with some information."

"Your wife is letting you speak to me again?"

There was a pause. "Sure. Hasn't she always?"

"She was a little miffed when I was calling you at home about the kidnappings."

"Ancient history. She knows that she's stuck with me forever."

"What do you need?"

"Some information about Dr. Rubenstein. He lives near your old home town, in Fond du Lac."

"He came after I moved out," Laurie said, "so I don't know too much. He treated my father for blood poisoning once. He seemed nice enough."

"Do you think he's pretty straight? Have you heard of him cutting any corners or involved in any funny stuff?"

"I assume that you have a specific incident in mind? In general, I don't know much about him. You know that the community up there is kind of small, and anything that anybody does is pretty common knowledge. So bad news travels quickly. All I know is that he's appointed. He got one of those deals where the Feds pay for part of his education and in return he's obligated to serve on a reservation or an economically depressed rural area for a few years."

"You said he got there after you moved away? So, he's been practicing there two or three years?"

"Yes, about that."

"Any complaints about him?"

Laurie paused and thought. "There was a rumor that he was at the bottom of his graduating class. I haven't heard that he's had a major malpractice problem or anything."

"We've got a missing woman from Sturgeon Lake," Dan said.

"It appears she was running a disorderly house out of her trailer. A couple of the customers claim they got exposed to gonorrhea and half the men in town ended up seeing Rubenstein for a shot of penicillin."

"Geez, Dan! A sex ring? In Pine County?"

Dan smiled. He could almost see Laurie's look of amusement. "Looks like it. I talked to Rubenstein. He claims the guys had chlamydia, but chlamydia isn't usually treated with penicillin."

"Um ... sounds like he was bought off by someone. Doesn't look like that big a deal, though."

"Maybe not, but I'd like to get the list of people who were treated," Dan said. "We think that one of the customers is tied to the disappearance, and we don't know who to talk to yet. The good doctor claims it's patient-doctor privilege and refuses to share anything without a court order."

"Sounds like he took a couple of arrogance classes, like most doctors I know." Laurie added, "I'd say that he's probably right, as much as it may piss you off."

"What do you know about Orrin Petrich?"

"Petrich?" Laurie asked. "The state senator?"

"Yeah. A neighbor put him at the woman's trailer earlier in the evening, but he won't talk to anyone. He threatened Al Jacobson, the mayor of Pine City, with a sewer condemnation and a cut off of state funding if Jacobson didn't pull me off his tail."

"I hear Petrich throws his weight around, a mover and a shaker. Not enough polish to ever be the majority leader or anything, but he's a man that can make things happen. I'd be careful. I'll bet he could burn your butt if he wanted to."

"Thanks for the warning. I think he's already got the match lit. Keep your ear to the ground and let me know if you hear anything."

"Sure," said Laurie.

. . .

Dan was dialing Tom Thompson's phone number when Pam Ryan stuck her head in his office. "Have you got a second, Dan?"

He hung up the phone. "Sure. What's up?"

Pam's eyes were red, and her short, blonde hair was mussed. She sat in Dan's guest chair and slid down. "We had an attempted murder near Duquette last night."

"A bar fight?"

Pam shook her head. "No. A Mrs. Ann Olsen was attacked in her house, on Highway 11. It looked like a botched burglary, but nothing was stolen. She was apparently clubbed with an old shotgun. The attacker was scared off when a Moose Lake squad responded to our call for assistance."

"Where were our squads?" Dan asked.

"I was nearly to the northwest corner of the county. Tom Thompson was west of Rock Creek. Mike Ronning responded from Moose Lake. He beat me to the scene by two or three minutes."

"You said the victim was Ann Olsen?"

Pam nodded.

Dan made a note, then asked, "How is she now?"

"I'm not sure," Pam replied. "After investigating the scene of the burglary, I drove over to the welding company, in Askov, to tell the victim's husband about the assault. Tom Thompson went to the Moose Lake emergency room to see if Mrs. Olsen was lucid enough to interview."

Dan fingered the note Thompson had left with the dispatcher. "I was just going to call Tom when you walked in. You said you didn't think it was a burglary?"

"No," Pam replied. "Nothing is missing. Ann Olsen's nightgown was pushed up around her waist after she was clubbed. It might have been an attempted rape."

"Let's call Tom and see what he knows." Dan dialed the phone number and switched on the speaker-phone so he and Pam could both listen."

"Thompson."

"Tom, this is Dan. I'm here with Pam Ryan on the speaker phone. Pam was updating me on the Olsen attack. Do you know anything new?"

"Hang on," Thompson replied. "I'm going to move outside." In a few seconds he was speaking again. "I spoke with the doctor and he says the victim has a concussion, but more importantly, her rectum was packed with some sort of substance that is acting like a depressant. He gave me a sample, It may be a barbiturate. He says the assailant knew enough to dose the victim rectally, hoping it wouldn't be found."

"Have you spoken with Mrs. Olsen yet?" Dan asked.

"She's just stabilizing now. The doctor says it may be hours before she's lucid."

"Is there any evidence she's been sexually assaulted?" Pam asked.

"He says it appears she wasn't sexually molested. The doctor was going to check on the presence of sperm when he found the powder."

"You said Eric Olsen came to the hospital," Dan said. "How is he doing?"

Thompson looked around to make sure no one was within earshot. "He seemed rattled, but not overwrought. If it had been my wife in this situation I would have been wild."

"Okay, Tom. You got anything else?"

"That's about it."

"Alright. Thanks, Tom. I think you and Pam should go home and get some rest."

Dan punched the button to turn off the speakerphone and leaned back. "I can't remember two months in a row when we've had assaults, much less two nights in a row. It's starting to be like Minneapolis around here."

Pam got up from the chair, hesitating at the door. "It is unusual. Do you think these cases are related?"

"I sure don't see what would link a bloody attack on a prostitute with an assault on a homemaker," Dan replied. "On the other hand, there aren't many sheer coincidences in police work."

"We didn't find many fingerprints at Olsen's house. The shotgun was wiped clean, except for some hairs. Is there anything I should do on that case tonight?"

"Get a day of sleep, then spend your shift at the hospital. See if she can remember anything. And keep an eye on her husband. Statistics say he's the most likely suspect, and Tom seems to think he's not reacting normally."

Chapter 12

Williams pulled out his notes on the Oinen investigation and a clean sheet of paper. He started a list of all the people that he knew who had frequented the trailer, and how they tied together. When he ran dry, he started a list of the things that he knew and the questions that he had. At the top of the list was the Franklin planner. Next to it was the note, "Where?"

He chose three names off the list and popped a Tums into his mouth as he headed out the door to make some visits.

The mayor of Sturgeon Lake owned the oil company. Williams caught him at the gas station, and in the course of questioning learned that he'd had prostate surgery that had left him impotent. He hadn't visited the trailer in a year. He did mention another name that Dan added to his list.

The next visit was to the veterinarian who worked out of his house between the towns of Sturgeon Lake and Willow River, along old Highway 61. Dan parked in the small lot behind the house and walked into the client entrance.

Ted Gapinski, D.V.M., was sitting behind the counter working on a computerized ledger when Williams walked in. They had known each other socially for fifteen years, since the doctor had moved to the area after practicing in Minneapolis for a few years.

"Dan. What brings you here? Must be the fine coffee we brew. Want a cup?"

"If it's fresh," said Dan, smiling. "The last stuff almost chipped a tooth."

Gapinski laughed as he poured them each a cup in ceramic mugs. "Come on into the office, Dan." He punched a few buttons on the computer as Williams walked by. "Got to save this file before I lose it."

"Ted, I suppose you heard about the assault in the trailer down by Sturgeon Lake?"

The Vet shook his head. "Nope, 'fraid not. Too much going on. Cows calving, horses with twisted stomachs, dogs hit by cars. It's been a couple of busy days."

"Well, Jean Oinen's trailer is covered with blood and there's no sign of her. We found tracks going down to the lake. The fire department has dragged, and we had some divers down, but can't find anything. The medical examiner says that there's enough blood there to indicate that the person doing the bleeding is dead."

"Wow!" Gapinski said. "That's a pretty nasty crime for this county. You got any suspects?"

"We've got a whole list. She was doing quite a bit of entertaining, and we've been collecting her customer list. Your name is on it."

The veterinarian face grayed, then he grinned sheepishly. "Well, if that's the case, I guess I might as well own up to making a few visits."

"Uh huh. You might as well, Ted. Now, I understand that the customers were a pretty close-knit group. No one got on the list without a referral. Who referred you?"

"I can't recall. I think it was one night at a poker party, and all the rest of the guys were joking about this great little set up that they had. We just got to talking about it and someone said, 'Teddy Boy, you ought to give it a try. It'll be the sweetest piece of ass you ever had.' I went for a visit and he was right."

"Who was at the poker party?"

"Oh, boy," the veterinarian said, as he rubbed his face thoughtfully. "That was almost three years ago. There were some who came and went, but we played with the same core group most of the time. Let's see. There was Rob Martin, the banker. Tommy Bergquist, from the towing service, was there. Ed Youngquist, who owns the resort on Sand Lake, and Elmer Swanson, the insurance man. I believe that's all."

"That was three years ago, you said?"

"Yeah. Two-and-a-half, maybe three years."

"Before the big outbreak of the clap?"

Gapinski looked away. "Yeah." His answer was almost inaudible. He leaned back in the chair and put his feet up on the desk. Sweat formed on his bald head and he drummed his fingers on the arm of his desk chair.

Williams waited in silence. Experience told him that there was a story to be shared. If he rushed ahead with another question, it might get buried.

After a minute, Gapinski looked back at the sheriff ruefully. His eyes were wet. "I screwed up real bad on that one, Dan.

When I got the word, I felt like a real shit. I had to tell Emily and own up to the whole mess. We went up to the doctor in Fond du Lac, the New York guy, and got tested. Then we both got a shot of penicillin." Gapinski's voice caught in his throat and he wiped his eyes.

After another minute, he found his voice again. "You got to promise not to spread this around, Dan."

Williams nodded.

"Emily reacted bad to the penicillin," continued Gapinski, "Anaphylaxis. Closed down her throat and respiratory system. I got her to the emergency room in Moose Lake quick as I could, but she died. I told everyone that it was a heart attack. I never went back to Jean's trailer after that. I couldn't face the stupid thing that I'd done." He picked a tissue from the box on his desk and blew his nose.

"Sorry, Ted. I didn't know. I had to know your connections."

"Sure. I understand. You're just doing your job."

"Can you think of anyone else connected to Jean?" Dan asked.

"Ah, not really. Jean was cagey. No one ever saw anyone else, far as I know. She must have kept a real good calendar and kept everything well-coordinated. She never talked about anyone else when I was there, either. She was great, like I was the only person in the world, when I was with her."

"All right, Ted. Thanks for the coffee."

. . .

At the Pine Brook Bank, Rob Martin said he didn't know Jean
Oinen or anything about the incident at the trailer, but Dan was-
n't buying it.

"Rob, she had to be one of your largest depositors. She had
several accounts with tens of thousands of dollars. Maybe a
safe-deposit box, too."

"Dan, I don't know my depositors personally. They come and
go out front while I deal with things in here."

"She was making several deposits a week. If I asked the
tellers if they knew her, would they recognize her?"

"They might. They might not."

"Were you bringing in the deposits for her and entering
them?"

Martin became visibly perturbed and got up from his chair.
He crossed to the door and pulled it closed.

"Dan, why are you doing this to me? Okay! Yes, I knew
Jeanie. I was a customer. I carried her deposits and put them on
the books to save her the trouble. But, Jesus, this could corrupt
the whole town. If people found out all the names who were
visiting a whore ... my God, we'd get thrown out of our church-
es. People would move their money out of the bank or take their
business to other stores. The whole town could be ruined." He
loosened the knot in his burgundy tie and unfastened the top
button of his white shirt.

"Maybe you should have thought of that before you started
dipping your pen in the community inkwell," said Williams.

"Twenty-twenty hindsight is great, isn't it?" the banker said sarcastically.

"Were you involved in the clap epidemic?"

"Thankfully, I wasn't. My wife was sick and I didn't have the opportunity to visit Jeanie for a couple of weeks. I heard it was quite a fiasco. Luckily, someone had the foresight to use the doctor up in Fond du Lac to keep the whole thing quiet."

"Yeah," Dan replied sarcastically. "That was really fortunate for you. Does Jean have a safe-deposit box here?"

"I wouldn't know."

Dan looked at Martin skeptically. "You knew about her accounts and you don't know whether she keeps a safety box?"

"I just deposited her money, that's all."

"Can you look it up?" Dan asked, knowing that he could.

"Of course." Martin started across the room and picked up a book. He started leafing through the pages until he found Jean Oinen's name. "She's got box number 213."

"When was the last time she was in it?"

The banker sighed heavily and picked up the phone. He dialed a three-digit extension. "Harry, when's the last time Jean Oinen was in her safe-deposit box?"

The banker listened for a moment. "All right, Harry, thanks." He hung up the phone and said, "She was in it about a week ago. Harry says she comes in weekly."

"Do you know what she keeps in it?"

"I have no idea. We have secure rooms where people take the boxes and add or remove materials privately."

"Hmmm. What size box does she have?"

Martin looked at the card. "The biggest we have. The size people have to store deeds, stock certificates, coins, old books and such."

"Maybe old diaries or appointment books?"

"They'd fit." Martin's face suddenly went ashen. "Oh, shit! You don't think … "

"Yes, I do, and I want it sealed, under orders from the sheriff. *No one* is to open that box. No one, do you understand? If anyone tries to get into it, I want a call put through on 911. You got that, Rob?"

Martin nodded, numbly.

Chapter 13

Williams drove back to the office and sat down at his desk. He pulled the Oinen customer list out of the lap drawer of his desk and penciled two more names onto the list. He put lines through the names of Ted Gapinski and Emil Amundson. He put a question mark next to Rob Martin's name. The banker had left him feeling a little uneasy.

He was prioritizing his afternoon visits when Floyd Swenson, Pine County's most experienced sergeant, popped his head through the door. "You interested in lunch?"

Floyd was the unofficial psychologist for the department, and Williams often used him as a discreet sounding board for ideas. "I'm not very hungry, but I might eat a piece of pie and talk for a while."

They sat in a booth looking out toward Main Street and talked as they ate. Dan reiterated the particulars of the Oinen case.

"I'm coming up dry on everyone but Petrich," Dan explained. "It seems like everyone I talk to really liked the girl. There's no motive buried anywhere that I can find."

"Dan, the thing that stands out for me is that someone apparently killed her, but they left thousands of dollars in a box by the door. Someone wanted her dead really bad, and the money was not the object."

"Yeah, that's the point. I can't find a motive and there are several questions I can't answer right now. For instance, why was there three-grand in an envelope with the number twenty-nine marked in the corner? There must be some significance there." Williams pulled out a notebook and made a note to himself to call the banker back and ask if any of the money he deposited ever came in a numbered envelope.

"Might be a date. Or, just an identifier," said Floyd.

"There's got to be something else, Floyd. I keep coming back to Petrich. All Jean's new clients were referred by other clients, except for Petrich. I haven't found anyone who knows how Petrich got into the circle. Maybe he wasn't even really a part of it. Maybe Jean was blackmailing him to keep his involvement quiet, and he killed her to shut her up … "

Floyd looked at his watch and frowned. "I've got two sets of papers to serve. I've got to hit the road." He picked up the check and threw a dollar on the table for a tip.

Williams took the check from his hand. "Let me pick this one up. I've got to get something else anyway."

Floyd grinned. "If you eat anymore Tums, your stomach is going to turn to cement. Why don't you go and see the doctor about your ulcer? Maybe he can fix it."

"Thanks, Mother Hen. But I just have a little heartburn." Dan threw some money on the table.

. . .

Dan walked back to the courthouse deep in thought. In his office, he stripped the wrapper from the new roll of Tums and popped two into his mouth. He looked over the list again and picked out three names that seemed unrelated to the others.

Williams drove north to Willow River, then west to a little town called Denham. Just north of the town, he pulled into a graveled parking area outside a construction trailer. The sign on the trailer said, "Bell Gravel and Concrete." Alongside the name was a logo showing a cracked Liberty Bell. It was a play on the owner's name. Williams opened the door and stepped inside. A young man was sitting at a table punching numbers into a computer.

"Excuse me, I'm looking for Ron Bell."

The young man swiveled around and looked at Williams. "I think he's out at the gravel pit. Hang on a second, I'll try to catch him on his cell-phone." He picked up a phone next to the computer and dialed a number. After a few seconds he spoke into the phone, then hung up. "You're lucky. He's pulling into the lot now."

From outside, Dan could hear the sound of tires on the gravel. Williams exited the trailer and met Ron Bell stepping out of his pickup. He was a slender but well built man in his early forties.

"Mr. Bell? I'm Dan Williams from the Pine County sheriff's department."

They shook hands and Bell motioned toward the door of the trailer.

"Maybe we should talk out here," said Dan. "It concerns Jean Oinen."

Bell's eyes grew wide for just an instant, then he quickly regained his composure. "What's the name again?"

"Sorry, Mr. Bell, but there's no use acting as though you don't know Jean. I got your name from Harry Nord. He said he'd referred you to her service."

Bell shook his head. "Well, thanks a ton, Harry. I hope your new driveway cracks this winter." He frowned and looked at Williams. "I heard about Jean. She's disappeared?"

"When was the last time you saw her?"

"I was there a couple of nights ago. Got there around five o'clock. Left about an hour after that. She was fine, then."

"Do you know who else was going to visit her that night?"

"No," Bell replied. "She was always very good about that. When I was with her it was like there weren't any others. I was never rushed, but we all knew when it was time to leave."

"So you didn't notice the other names in her planner?"

"What planner?" A hint of anxiety had entered Bell's voice.

"She kept a planning book, like a diary. That's how she kept track of all the comings and goings."

"I had no idea. I guess that I never thought about it."

"What time did you leave?"

"Well, like I said, about six," Bell replied. "I went home and had supper and then watched television the rest of the evening. My wife can vouch for me."

"Who referred you to Jean originally?"

Bell paused for a second too long before responding. "Harry Nord. We fish some together, and he put me onto his set-up when things got a little tense at home for me."

Dan made a mental note to draw only a dotted line from Nord to Bell on his graph. "Have you made any referrals?"

Bell's lips tightened. "I don't believe so."

Williams hesitated and let the silence work on Bell.

"No. As a matter of fact, I never did," he said.

"Did you get caught up in the clap incident?"

Bell laughed. "You've done your homework, Sheriff. Yes, I had my penicillin shot from the witch doctor's nurse."

"If you think of the names of any other clients that Jean had, please give the sheriff's department a call and leave me a message."

. . .

Bell walked into the trailer and watched Williams pull out of the lot. "Tommy, take a break."

"But I've got this spreadsheet on cement loading running ..."

"I said take a break. Get out of here for a while. I need to make a call."

The younger man moved the computer mouse around and saved the file he was working on, then he left the trailer, muttering. Bell dug through his wallet and pulled out a card for a diesel-parts supplier. He flipped it over and dialed the St. Paul phone number penciled on the back. The phone rang three times before the female voice answered.

"Get me the senator."

"I'm sorry, sir, but he's in conference right now. May I take a message and have him get back to you later?"

"No. I need to talk to the senator, *now*. Tell him Ron Bell is on the line with an emergency."

"I'll see what I can do, sir."

The line clicked as the hold button was pushed, followed by a quiet hum. Within thirty seconds, the female voice was back. "The senator is finishing his meeting now and will be right with you."

Orrin Petrich did not sound pleased when he came on the line. "Bell, why the hell are you calling me? What's the emergency?"

"The Pine County sheriff's department was just here asking about Jean."

"Shit! What did you tell them?"

"That I was a customer. That I'd been there a couple of nights ago. That I'd had the clap and a shot of penicillin."

"Why'd you tell them all that?" Petrich asked. "Why admit any more than you have to?"

"He knew it all," Bell replied. "I was just confirming what was already on the books. I didn't mention your name, or any others, so I think that you're in the clear."

"No, I'm not clear. The son-of-a-bitch called here yesterday. I told him to fuck off. I also threatened the Pine City mayor if he couldn't get the sheriff's boys off my backside."

"I don't like it, Senator. They're sniffing too close."

"Just stay cool. They haven't connected us to anything."

"That's easy for you to say. They have an envelope with my fingerprints and lots of money. If they ever put that together, they'll be back. By the way, did you know that Jeanie kept a diary or some kind of appointment book?"

"WHAT?" Petrich exclaimed. "No wonder he's finding all of

us. We've got to get that out of his hands. That's dynamite with the fuse lit. Do you have any idea how much is in it?"

"No. I didn't know anything about it. The cop mentioned it in passing."

"Can you arrange to have it removed?"

"What?" Bell asked. "You want me to have something stolen from the *sheriff's department*?"

"Not stolen. Just lost. Doesn't the sheriff share a building with Public Works? Maybe one of your contacts could lift it over lunch. Got anyone that owes you big?"

Bell hesitated as he considered his options. "I don't like this, Petrich."

"Do you like the prospect of a few years behind bars any better?"

"Shit! Dammit!"

"Don't sweat it, Bell. All you have to do is make that diary disappear. I have some friends who will get this out of the sheriff's jurisdiction. The Pine County good-ole-boys will be off this case soon. Trust me."

. . .

Williams visited two more of Jean's clients in the afternoon. Both were upstanding citizens. One hadn't been to the trailer in several months, and the other broke down in tears at the news that some harm might have come to Jean. They both supplied him with two more names, and a repeat of Ted Gapinski, the veterinarian.

Williams crossed both of them off the list, but left a little star next to Ron Bell's name. He popped two more Tums and then drove home for supper. Sally was reading a Harlequin romance novel on the couch when he pulled in the driveway. She met him at the door with her coat on.

"I thought that we'd go out for supper," Sally suggested.

"Any place in particular?"

"Not as long as you're treating."

They drove east, toward Sturgeon Lake. "Any breakthrough on the missing hooker?" Sally asked.

"Lots of circles and questions. I put X's next to a lot of leads, and question marks next to others."

"Still no body?"

"Nothing," Dan replied. "The fire department dragged the lake and had some divers down. Personally, I suspect that she's in a shallow grave in the woods someplace. Maybe some hunter will find her this fall. If she's in the lake, she'll float up when the weather warms up."

"Still chasing lots of big shots?"

"Yes. But I'm still not ready to tell you names. A lot of them are already living in their private little hell over this."

They drove in silence for a while before Sally said, "Ted Gapinski is one of them. The emergency room doctor dropped off some notes to be typed. He told me that Ted's wife died after getting a penicillin shot for gonorrhea. That's what you were talking about last night, wasn't it?"

Dan smiled. "My very own detective."

"I guess it was terrible," Sally added. "Ted rushed her in after giving her a shot of epinephrine at home, but her throat just closed down until she had a heart attack. The doctor said there was nothing he could do to save her. Ted was at her side until her heart finally couldn't be revived. I guess he was pretty rattled."

"Ted still had a hard time talking about it this morning. He was practically in tears. Has the rumor mill at the clinic picked up on the Pine County crime wave?"

"What crime wave?" Sally asked as they pulled into the parking lot at Mister Ed's place.

"We had another assault, out near Duquette. We didn't have a squad close by, so Moose Lake took the call, with Pam Ryan backing up. A woman was clubbed during a burglary."

"That's bad," Sally said. "Did they catch the burglar?"

Dan held the door open and said, "Not yet."

. . .

Thomas Gray, the Minnesota state attorney general, was reading the *St. Paul Dispatch* after dinner when the phone rang.

"Tom, Orrin Petrich here. I have a problem."

"Hello, Senator. What's the problem?" the AG asked.

"Well, here's the situation. The Pine County sheriff's department is investigating the disappearance of a prostitute. They think she may have been murdered, but they don't have a body or a suspect."

"And how's that a problem for you, Orrin?"

"They have a witness that mistakenly thinks I was there shortly before the disappearance. Now they're harassing me and one of my associates."

"And you have nothing to do with the matter?"

"Nothing. My conscience is clear on the matter."

"What do you have in mind?"

"I'd like you to bury it. Take the case and put it where the sun doesn't shine."

"Orrin, it would be highly irregular for the AG office to step into a county investigation like this."

"Dammit, Tom, I know that! I'm just too busy right now to have to fool with crap like this. Now, can you take care of it?"

"Orrin, you know I can't ... ."

"For Christ sake, Tom! Let me remind you, it would also be highly irregular for your constituents to know that the AG was once in a little trouble with a DWI. How would it look when the next election came up if that little tidbit came out in the newspapers? Huh? Especially the part about a state trooper getting a choice assignment driving the governor after he declined to issue a ticket or file a report."

"Orrin, how many times am I going to pay for that little indiscretion? Two, three or a hundred times?"

"This isn't a high price, Tom. All I want you to do is bury the investigation of the disappearance of a prostitute. Who is going to give a rat's ass about that? You might find that the local businessmen that paid her visits will probably be relieved."

There was a long silence. When Petrich was about to speak again, he heard Gray heave a long, resigned sigh.

"Okay, Orrin. One more time. I'll make some inquiries tomorrow. But, I can't make any guarantees. Things like this have a way of getting out of hand."

Chapter 14

Dan Williams pulled off the freeway at the Willow River exit and took a sharp right into the parking lot of the restaurant and gas station. The low building, with dirty bricks, wasn't flashy enough to attract the freeway travelers, but it was a favorite hangout for the locals. Dan took a table near the window.

When the stubby owner, Randy Bjork, came by with a cigarette dangling from his lip, Dan asked him to sit down.

"What's up, Dan?" Randy asked.

"Did you hear about Jean Oinen?"

"I heard there was something going on at her place, that she might be missing."

"She is missing, and we found blood all over the place."

"Oh, my God! Jean's or somebody else's?" Bjork asked.

"We don't know yet. The medical examiner said that there was enough loss of blood to kill anyone."

Bjork shook his head in dismay and then rubbed a hand over the day-old growth of black beard. He sat down across from Dan and stubbed out his cigarette. "I can't believe anything's happened to Jeanie," he said. "She was a great gal."

"I've heard that same thing from a lot of her customers," said Dan. He waited for a moment. "I understand that you were one of'em."

Randy's eyes narrowed. He leaned back in the booth and fished a pack of Marlboro's from his shirt pocket. He lit the cigarette and inhaled deeply, squinting as he blew out a heavy plume of smoke. "Okay, Dan. Okay. Emil Amundson warned me that you'd be by. Yeah, like I said, she was a great gal."

"Have you been to Jean's trailer lately?" Williams watched Randy's face closely for any sign of equivocation. Randy looked around nervously, then he leaned forward. "Yeah. Last week. One night. I haven't been going too much 'cause my wife has been getting a little suspicious."

"What can you tell me about her appointment book?"

"Oh, well, I guess I knew that she had one. I never saw it, or talked with her about it."

"Were you involved in the clap epidemic, Randy?" Dan asked.

Randy frowned and gritted his teeth. "Ouch! Looks like you know it all. Yeah, I had my penicillin shot."

"Anyone ever say who brought it into the group?"

Randy looked around and, seeing no one close, leaned back in the booth again. "We all speculated that it was the politician. I don't even know his name. But Jeanie and Ann sure complained about him after that episode."

Williams froze for a second and wondered who "Ann" was. Then he remembered the discussion with Pam Ryan that morning. Wasn't the Olsen woman named Ann? Thinking quickly, he said, "Ann doesn't seem to know where Jean is, either."

"I haven't seen Ann in over a year. I don't think she and Jean have been close for a while." Bjork hesitated, then asked, "Dan, are we in trouble over this? I mean, are all of us going to get our names in the paper, or dragged into court?"

Dan shook his head. "I doubt it," he replied, "unless you're the one who made the bloody mess in the trailer." Again, Dan watched Randy's face carefully.

"Dan, believe me, I don't know of anyone, including me, who would harm Jeanie. She was great. Even if there was some problem, we'd all probably just pitch in to help her, anyway we could." He looked down, shaking his head.

"Alright, Randy. I hope you're right. In the meantime, stay around here, close. I may need to talk to you again. And, don't worry, I'll try to keep this as quiet as possible."

A look of relief crossed Randy's face. "Thanks, Sheriff. Good luck. You know that most of us will help any way we can."

"Say, Randy. Do you know if Ann's last name is Olsen?"

Bjork shrugged. "You know, I don't know if I ever knew her last name. Is it important?"

"Just checking."

. . .

Williams trusted his intuition as to whether a person was lying or telling the truth, and his intuition told him to cross Bjork off the list. In the meantime, he kept coming back to the question as to whether Bjork's mention of the name "Ann" referred to Ann Olsen.

Back in his office, Dan pulled out the lap drawer of his desk and searched for his list. The drawer was in more than its usual state of disarray, and he couldn't locate the list. He walked out to the dispatcher's cube.

"Lois, has anyone been looking in my desk for something?"

"Not that I know about, Dan."

"Any strangers around?"

"No, haven't seen anyone."

Dan stopped by John Sepanen's office, but it was empty. There was no sign of his list on the Sheriff's desk.

The ready room was empty, with only the usual litter of mail and notes on the desks of the deputies. No sign of his list. He went back to his office and reconstructed it from his notes. Luckily, he carried them around with him.

He picked out two more names and headed out for interviews.

. . .

The phone in the construction trailer rang.

"Is Ron Bell around?"

"Yeah, just a second." The surveyor handed the phone to Ron. "Hello?"

"Ron," a male voice said, "I went through ... ah ... the office we spoke about. I couldn't find a diary or anything like that. I picked up a piece of paper with a bunch of names on it. Your name had a star next to it. A lot of them had the names crossed out. I can put it in the mail to you."

"No, just touch a match to it. But there was no sign of the diary? Did you check everywhere?"

"I went through every desk drawer and file cabinet," the man replied. "If it's there I don't know what it looked like. And let me tell you, I was sweating bullets. If anyone had caught me I'd be in deep donkey dung."

"Anywhere else it might be?" Bell asked.

"If they picked it up at the trailer it might be in the property room. They log all evidence and keep it there for trials."

"Can you check it out?"

"Are you serious? We're talking heavy security there! That's where they store all the drugs and money they confiscate. Everyone who goes in or out of the property room signs a log. They have a surveillance camera that runs all the time. It's like Fort Knox. No way they'll let a stinking contract employee in the engineer's office in there. I've got no need to be there."

"Okay. You'll be appropriately rewarded for your efforts and we'll let you know if there are other opportunities."

"I don't want anymore opportunities! You can take your opportunities and shove them. This isn't my line of work, Ron."

"Too late for that. You volunteered once. You ever hear the old saying, in for an inch, in for a mile?"

"Dammit, Ron, I don't want any more of this. I can't take it."

"Don't worry. Everything's going to be fine. I'll get back to you."

. . .

Williams stopped off and questioned two more of the individuals whose names were on the list. Those two gave him names, but they were repeats of names he already had, although he did find one more referral connection. When he asked them about "Ann," they referred to her in the past tense, and neither of them knew her last name. He crossed both of these men off his list. He still hadn't found the person who had referred Orrin Petrich.

Dan decided to stop off at the Pine City Hospital. After a short visit with the receptionist he went to patient records. Pat Reynolds, the records clerk and an old friend, offered to check for any records they might have on Jean Oinen. She didn't find any.

"Can I take a look at Emily Gapinski's file?" Dan asked.

"I can't think of any reason why not," said Pat. "Sure. Hold on just a minute. I'll see what we have."

Within a few minutes she was back with an expandable folder that had a series of colored tags on the end. "You can look at this at the desk over there."

Williams sat in silence, reading through several years of tests, x-rays and medical reports. He came to the records from Emily's last visit. It was an assortment of test results, most of which held little meaning for him. He found the emergency room physician's report and read through it.

The report stated, in objective terms:

The patient was delivered to the hospital by her husband, Theodore Gapinski, in a state of severe respiratory distress. The husband had reported that she'd received a massive dose of penicillin to treat an infection. The penicillin injection had been administered by the nurse in Dr. Rubenstein's office, in Fond du Lac, Minnesota, earlier that afternoon. The husband reported that the patient started to exhibit classic signs of an allergic reaction to the penicillin within half an hour of returning home. Itching and hives were evident. She reportedly took 50 mg. of Benadryl orally at the onset of the hives, without relief. After approximately one hour, respiratory distress was starting to be manifested. The patient's husband, a Dr. of Veterinary Medicine, administered epinephrine, sub-Q, from his veterinary supplies, at home. When the respiratory distress worsened, he delivered her to the emergency room. The patient was having great difficulty breathing. Her consciousness was impaired from apparent oxygen deprivation and I intubated her. The patient's temperature was 103F. More epinephrine was administered, but the respiratory system was nearly at a state of collapse. The patient's skin started to discolor, indicating the onset of hemolysis, and cardiac arrest set in within minutes. Efforts to resuscitate were unsuccessful and the patient was declared dead at 5:13 p.m.

The last item in the file was a receipt from the Cremation Society of Minnesota. Their transport had picked up the body the following day. There were no other reports in the file.

Williams carried the file to the desk. "Pat, did they do an autopsy on Emily Gapinski?"

"If they did," Reynolds said, "it should be in the file. When someone dies in the hospital, they sometimes don't. It's up to the family most times."

"Thanks." Dan handed the file back to Pat and walked out.

. . .

At the courthouse Dan checked for messages, and then

stopped off in Sheriff Sepanen's office. At his light knock, Sepanen looked up from a stack of papers on his desk.

"Hi, Dan, how are things going? What can I do for you?"

"John, I think someone rifled through my desk this morning."

"What makes you think so?"

"They went through all the desk drawers and the file cabinet drawers and left things a little messed up. The only thing that I can see that's missing is the list of names that I had from the Oinen investigation and a few notes that I had on the back of a sheet of paper."

The sheriff settled back in his chair. "You think someone is trying to mess up the investigation?"

"I don't know, but it's a little too much of a coincidence that we get all kinds of pressure to ease off the investigation, then someone comes in and steals my notes and a list of suspects. Don't you think?"

"You and I both know about so-called 'coincidences,' Dan. What's missing?" the sheriff asked. "Just a list of names?"

"Good question," Dan replied. "The list is the only thing I've noticed so far."

"Has anyone strange been wandering around?"

"The dispatcher sees everyone that comes and goes," Dan said. "The day-deputies didn't see anyone. But it could have been someone last night, or even yesterday afternoon."

"Can you lock your desk and file cabinet?"

"I shouldn't have to lock anything with the control we have on people entering this area."

"Obviously, that isn't enough," the sheriff said. "You sure it wasn't one of our own people looking for something?"

"Can't think of anything they'd be looking for. Lois didn't see anyone around my office."

"Well, you better start locking the Oinen stuff up. Better check the property room to see if anyone has been in the evidence from that investigation, too."

"Good idea," Dan said. "I think I'll take a run back to the trailer to see if anything's been disturbed there. Oh, I told Rob Martin to seal Jean Oinen's safe-deposit box at the Pine Brook bank."

"What would you be looking for there?"

"She has the largest box you can get. I suspect she has some records on her clients locked away, maybe as insurance. She kept some sort of daily records, and maybe her old records are in there."

"Blackmail might be a strong murder motive for the right person," the sheriff noted. "Are you going to get a court order to open it?"

"I'm not getting anywhere the way we're going. I think we should."

"Put together a request and I'll take it to a judge."

"One other gem." Dan said. "Jean apparently used to have a partner. Everyone says they aren't close anymore. But I sure would like to talk to her."

"What's her name?" the sheriff asked.

"Ann something."

"Hard to look her up in the phone book. Too many 'Somethings' listed."

"Right," said Dan, ignoring the sheriff's attempt at humor. "Might be Ann Olsen, but I'm not sure."

"Well, that narrows it down a little," said the sheriff, grinning.

. . .

Dan walked to the property room and checked in with the clerk. After receiving assurances no one had touched the Oinen-case evidence, he got the location and found the box sitting on an open shelf.

Inside were a number of things: the envelope with the number 29 in the corner; a receipt for the money from the cedar box; some papers; and a ring of six keys. Two of the keys looked like deposit-box keys and one was stamped with the name of the Pine Brook State Bank and the number 213. He removed it from the ring and put the box back on the shelf. At the clerk's desk, he signed a receipt for the key.

In his office, he dug through his desk drawer and found the keys for the file cabinet. He dropped the deposit box key into the top file drawer, and locked the cabinet. He slid the file cabinet key onto his key ring and dropped it into his pocket. "That's as safe as I can make it," he said to himself. He then scribbled a list of the things he wanted to search for in Jean Oinen's bank box and handed the note to Norma Kostroskie, the clerk.

"Norma, could you type me out a court order for these things, then give it to Sheriff Sepanen?"

"Sure, Dan," said Norma, scanning the note.

"Thanks," said Dan.

Outside, he slid in behind the wheel of the unmarked squad, started the engine, and headed toward the blood-smeared trailer by Sturgeon Lake.

Chapter 15

The blue pickup truck wheeled up the exit ramp at Barnum and made a right turn, followed by another quick right that took it down the frontage road a quarter-mile to the boat launch. It took the driver two attempts to get the Shorelander boat trailer lined up with the launch. He backed slowly, watching the wheels disappear into the water.

The fishing boat slid easily off the trailer, tugging at the bow rope. A cold north wind pushed the boat sideways as the man pulled it towards the short dock. This cold snap would keep all but the most serious fishermen off the lake on days like this.

He tied the boat to the dock and pulled the truck and trailer into the empty parking lot. He pulled the Gore-tex and Thinsulate parka from behind the seat and was putting it on as he walked back to the dock. In the boat, he turned the key in the dash. The Evinrude engine coughed, sputtered, and died.

"Come on, baby. Hang in there."

A second attempt yielded the same result. On the third try, the engine spewed a cloud of blue smoke and rumbled to life. The man squeezed the throttle handle and eased it back. The engine slowed slightly as the propeller dug into the water and pushed the boat away from the dock.

In the middle of the lake, he turned the bow of the boat quartering into the waves, washing from the northeast. He headed toward a Carlton County park a quarter-mile from the boat launch. When he got near the park, he slipped the throttle back to the top neutral position and switched off the engine. The waves pushed at the side of the boat and it started to roll gently as he pulled a fishing rod from the rack on the side of the stowage compartment.

He rigged a small jig on the end of the line and tossed it over the side. The motion of the boat pulled the line out and he leaned back into the seat. The sun was just disappearing behind the hill to the west when he felt a tiny tug on the line. He gave the fishing rod a quick twitch and felt the pull of the fish on the line.

"Damn!"

He reeled in the ten-inch crappie and looked at it in the water, trying to decide whether to give the rod a quick snap and rip the jig free of the fish's mouth, or to take it in. He elected to lift it into the boat. After slipping the hook from its mouth he opened the lid to a live well and dropped it in. He cast the jig back into the water and flipped a switch on the console. A pump hummed to life, pumping fresh water into the live well.

He felt a slow pull on the rod and turned to look over his shoulder. The water was getting shallow and his jig pulled and tugged at the sparse weeds that were near the island. He tugged it free once, then reeled the jig in. As the boat drifted behind the small island, Interstate-35 and the houses at the north end of the lake disappeared from sight.

He pushed a button, marked *trim,* and with a hum, the motor tipped up so that only the propeller was in the water. He turned the key and pushed the throttle ahead. With a crunch, the bow of the boat pushed against the sandy gravel on the island shore. The motor died.

He walked to the bow and jumped onto the shore. With one pull, the boat moved another two feet further aground. He got quickly back into the boat, and in the far stern he pulled at the tarpaulin that covered the naked body, the reason for this rather unusual fishing expedition. He dragged the tarpaulin and its contents between the seats, then rolled it over the bow onto the shore.

On shore, he dragged the tarpaulin out of the shore grass and into the edge of the brush. Once there, he unrolled the tarp, revealing the woman's body inside. He carried the tarp back to the boat and looked around for the shovel. He stopped suddenly, remembering the shovel sitting in the back of the pickup bed. He had forgotten to get it. He couldn't believe it.

"Damn!"

He gave the tarp a quick rinse in the lake water, then threw it into the boat and walked back. In five minutes he had gathered a myriad of sticks and marsh grass, using them to cover the body. The sweat dripped from the man's forehead as he trudged back toward the boat. He stopped and looked again at the spot where Jean Oinen had found her final resting place. The body might have surfaced later, in the lake. Here, she would never be found. Job well done, he thought, even without the shovel.

Back at the boat, he pushed it away from shore, stepped in,

and started the motor. Once out into the lake, he threw out his jig, and headed back toward the launch. If anyone were watching, no one would be surprised that a person would give up after only thirty minutes on a day like this. Even fishermen yielded to common sense sometimes.

. . .

The trailer was dark and the lock on the door was secure. The yellow crime-scene tape across the door seemed undisturbed. Williams pulled the tape back and unlocked the door. The smell of the drying blood rushed to his nostrils and he had to look away for a few seconds until he became used to it.

Inside, the trailer looked as it had when he saw it for the first time. He moved quietly, poking in drawers in the hope of finding the one thing the investigating deputies had missed. He didn't.

He pulled a chair up to the desk in the bedroom and sat down, staring at the items strewn across the surface: a gold pen; a gold paper clip, holding a number of bills; open envelopes with bills; a couple of tiny sample vials of perfume; a plastic ruler, and a bookmark.

"Jean, where is your diary?" Dan said to himself. He pulled open the desk drawer and looked at the array of paper clips, push pins, staple puller, and pens. Farther back was a white envelope, still gray with fingerprint dust. Inside the envelope was an old picture of a couple Dan didn't recognize, standing in front of a Ford, seventies vintage. The man, dressed in a suit, was a younger and trimmer version of Jean's father. The second picture was of two little girls. The first picture had nothing on the back to indicate who the people were. The second had a note in faded blue ink: "Annie and Jeanie, June 1986."

"Same Ann?" Dan asked himself. "Maybe."

When he reached to put the picture back he saw a business card that had been hidden under the envelope. It showed the name of a lawyer in Hinckley. "Another customer?"

He dropped the card in his pocket and put two more Tums in his mouth to stop the burning in his belly. After he locked the door to the trailer, he turned and saw a face peeking out between the mini-blinds in the trailer next door. He walked over and knocked on the door. The door opened tentatively and Vera Youngquist peered around the edge.

"Hello, Mrs. Youngquist. Dan Williams, from the sheriff's office. May I ask you a couple of questions?"

"Hello, Sheriff. Come on in."

Williams stepped inside.

"Cup of coffee, Sheriff?" asked Vera Youngquist.

"No, thanks, ma'am. I just need to ask a couple of questions and be on my way. Have you seen anyone snooping around here since the night Jean disappeared?" he asked.

"Only you," she replied. "But we *have* been keeping an eye out. I have your license number written down and if anyone had asked, I would have given it to them."

Dan smiled. "Mrs. Youngquist," he said, "tell me about Jean's friend, Ann."

The woman thought for a moment. "Ann?" she asked, shaking her head. "I remember another girl that was around for a while, but I don't remember ever hearing her name. She was a tiny thing, with blonde hair."

. . .

Williams drove home and pulled in the driveway just behind Sally.

"Short day today?" she asked as she stepped out of the car.

"Yeah," Dan laughed, "only ten hours."

They walked in together. "What culinary delight do you have planned for us this evening?" he asked.

"How does Dinty Moore beef stew strike you?"

"Fits right in with the rest of the day," he replied. "Kind of a disappointment."

"No progress?"

"Some," he said. "I now know that Jean Oinen used to have a partner."

"Hey!" Sally said cheerily. "We're talking a prostitution ring here. This is big stuff. Any progress on the other assault?"

"Haven't had much time to pursue it. I told Pam Ryan to spend the night there and see if the victim had anything to say. There is one interesting sidelight: Jean's partner and the victim were both named Ann."

"You don't believe much in coincidences." Sally said.

"I know, but what are the odds a woman with a little kid, living in Duquette, was a prostitute's partner in Sturgeon Lake? I don't think so."

"Do you think the partner, whoever she is, would be able to help with the investigation?"

"I don't think so. The two have been apart for a year or more.

But I'd like to find her. She may know something more than the customers." Dan paused, then added, "And someone rifled through my desk today."

"Your desk? In the courthouse?" she asked.

"Yeah," Dan said, "they took a list of Jean's customers. Luckily, I could reconstruct it from my notes. About the only other progress was crossing three more names off the list and finding the name of another customer in Hinckley."

"Too bad real investigations don't go like they do on television."

"Yeah. Right."

Chapter 16

On his way to visit the lawyer in Hinckley, Williams stopped off for breakfast at Banning Junction, along I-35. The sun was rising and starting to melt the frost from the grass as he walked to the parking lot after breakfast. He started the car and popped two Tums to counteract the effects of the fried eggs and coffee.

The drive from Banning Junction to Hinckley was quiet in the early morning. He met a few trucks hauling loads to Duluth. A ruffed grouse flew from the birch and aspen forest that lined the highway, and crossed just above his windshield.

Williams turned west from the freeway and drove into the older downtown section of Hinckley, away from the new development around the freeway exit and the sprawling casino another mile to the east.

Downtown, he found the lawyer's office. It was in an old building, dating back to the building boom after the great fire of 1894. The lawyer's name and profession, *William Peikert Attorney*, were painted on a second-story window overlooking the street.

Williams knocked once before opening the door and entering. Inside, an old man sat at a desk that faced the door. The man would have looked very much in place if he'd been wearing a green eyeshade and arm bands, like an old time accountant.

"May I help you?" Peikert asked.

Williams walked toward the desk offering his hand. "Dan Williams, from the Pine County sheriff's Department."

Peikert rose from his chair and shook hands. "Please, have a seat." He gestured toward an oak desk chair without any padding. It seemed that Peikert wasn't too concerned for his clients' comfort. Williams sat down.

"What can I do for you, Sheriff?" asked Peikert.

"I'm investigating a crime, and I found your business card at the scene." Williams handed him the card. "I was wondering if you could tell me about your connection with Jean Oinen?"

Peikert took the card and looked at it briefly before handing it back. "Certainly. I was doing some research for Miss Oinen."

"Could you tell me the nature of that research?"

"I'm afraid not, unless she gave her permission. She wanted it to be very discreet. I think that's one of the reasons that she didn't use a lawyer closer to her residence. Is Miss Oinen in some sort of trouble?"

"I take it you aren't aware of the incident at her trailer?"

The lawyer shook his head.

"We believe there was an assault there a few days ago, and someone was badly injured, if not killed. We don't know the identities of the parties involved, but we assume that Jean Oinen was one of them. She has not been seen since that night."

The lawyer leaned forward and made a steeple with his hands

while resting his elbows on the desk. "Oh, dear. That does make things difficult. I suppose you think you need to know the nature of the work I was doing in case it might be tied to her disappearance?"

"That's the general idea," Dan replied.

"Hmmm. Let's see. Well, I can say that she was trying to locate a missing person. Beyond that I was doing some contract work for her, and setting up a will."

Dan leaned forward. "Can you tell me who the missing person is? Would it be her former partner, Ann?"

"I'm afraid that's confidential," Peikert replied. "She would not want that revealed, and I don't want to play twenty-questions with you."

"Can you tell me who the beneficiary of the will is?"

"Hmmm. I guess there's no harm in saying that it is the missing person."

"Is her estate large?"

"I'm not privy to her full financial situation. I was left with the impression that it was not immense, but large enough to cause her concern about its disposition."

"She has a large safe-deposit box in the Pine Brook Bank," Dan said. "Do you have any idea what's in it?"

The lawyer leaned back in his chair again. "Sheriff, I don't mean to appear overly suspicious, but it has just occurred to me that you haven't provided me any identification. Could I see your identification please?"

Williams reached into his jacket pocket and pulled the badge case out. He opened it, exposing the badge with his picture, and handed it to the lawyer.

"From the way you're talking," the lawyer said, as he studied Dan's photo, "I'm led to believe that my client is assumed to be deceased?" He handed the badge and case back.

"The medical examiner says someone lost enough blood to have died. We don't know who the victim was. As I said, there has been no sign of Jean Oinen in several days."

The lawyer smoothed his hair with one hand. "Well, in answer to your question, I can speculate she might have some investment papers stored in the safe-deposit box. Beyond that I can't say what it might contain. I am not privy to the contents."

"Do you know what business she's in?"

"She's my client. I'm not at liberty to discuss the nature of her businesses."

"I know she was a prostitute," Dan stated directly. "I've interviewed a good share of her clientele."

The lawyer nodded without speaking.

"Can you expand beyond that?" Dan asked.

"Not really. We didn't discuss the exact nature of her business, although I have made some deductions about it from our conversations."

"You can't offer me any more than that?"

Peikert drew a deep breath and sighed, as if he were tiring of the conversation. "Not without her permission, or until I know she's dead."

"We'd like to open her safe-deposit box. I believe there may be evidence there that will lead us to a motive and perhaps a suspect."

Peikert shook his head. "I'm afraid I would have to fight any move to do that until I know whether she is alive or dead. If she's alive, I'm sure that she would not want the box opened to inspection."

Williams frowned. "You don't want to assist us in determining what happened?"

Peikert leaned back in his chair. "That's not at all the case. I just think that my client's interests wouldn't be served by opening that box, if she is alive."

"Were you one of her customers?"

The lawyer smiled slightly. "You flatter me, Sheriff. I'm an old man, and I have found comfort with my wife for nearly forty years. I don't need that kind of excitement at this point in my life."

Dan smiled. "Do you know who any of her customers were?"

The lawyer stared Williams in the eye. "I'm afraid that would fall under the category of lawyer-client privilege, even if I did know."

"But Mr. Peikert; what if one of them killed her?"

"It's an easy problem to solve. You prove that she's dead, and I may be able to help. If she's alive, I could be incriminating her and several other people who may or may not be clients."

Williams walked out of the office and to the unmarked squad parked in front of the pawnshop.

"Damned lawyers!" He muttered under his breath as he unlocked the car and climbed in.

. . .

At his desk Dan pushed aside a note to call Pam Ryan, assuming that she was already asleep after her night shift at the hospital. Instead, he started to rewrite the list of clients. Suddenly, he had an idea. He pulled out a clean sheet of paper and started a sociogram, linking each client with his referring friend and the new people he had, in turn, referred. When he had finished, at the bottom of the list was Orrin Petrich's name with no lines connecting it to any of the others.

On a separate sheet, he started listing unanswered questions:

Who referred Petrich?
Was there a murder?
Is Jean Oinen still alive?
If dead, where is the body?
Who was Jean Oinen trying to find?
What's in the safety deposit box?
Do I have all the clients?
Where's the diary/planner?
If Petrich is innocent, why is he avoiding questioning?
What is Jean's blood type?
Where, why and when did Jean Oinen get a transfusion?

He tapped his pencil on the desktop a few more times. Then he scribbled two last questions:

Who's "Annie," in the picture?
Is Ann Olsen the partner?

He dug through a drawer to find a Moose Lake phone directory and looked up the phone number for the Moose Lake Gas Station and General Repair. The woman who answered the phone said she'd get Elmer Oinen from the back.

"Hello?"

"Mr. Oinen. This is Dan Williams from the Pine County sher-iff's department. I stopped at your trailer the other morning. I have a couple more questions."

"Still no sign of Jeanie?" Oinen asked.

"Not yet. We got samples of blood from the trailer and we're trying to figure out if it belongs to Jean. Has she ever been hos-pitalized, like for an appendectomy or something?"

"Not that I remember," Oinen replied. "She had a broken arm once. We took her to Mercy hospital for that."

"What's your blood type?"

"Mine's O-positive."

"Do you know what Jean's mother's blood type was?"

"Sorry. No idea."

"Jean was looking for a missing person. Do you have any idea who she was trying to find?"

"No. I can't think of anyone. There are a few cousins she has-n't seen in a few years. But she hasn't been close to any of the family in a long time. My wife died years ago, so it's not her."

"I found a couple of old pictures in the trailer," Dan said. "One is of a young couple all dressed up, standing next to an old Ford car, looks like seventies model. The picture doesn't say anything on the back. The other one says Jean and Annie, June 1986. Do you know who the people would be?"

"Annie is easy. Annie Hapka was Jean's best friend for years. The other picture sounds like my wedding picture. I know Jean had a copy of it, once."

Williams scribbled notes quickly. "Is Annie Hapka still

around Moose Lake?"

"Sure," Oinen replied. "I see her once in awhile. She works at the dime store."

"Thanks, Mr. Oinen."

"Say, Deputy Williams?" Oinen's voice sounded unsure. "If you find out something, you will call me, won't you?"

"I wasn't sure you were interested."

"I wasn't sure, either. But I am. Okay?"

"I'll let you know, Mr. Oinen. Thanks again."

Williams looked up the number for the Moose Lake Ben Franklin store, called the "dime store" by old-timers.

"Ben Franklin store, may I help you?" The voice was female, and sounded very young.

"This is Dan Williams, from the Pine County sheriff's department. I would like to speak with Annie Hapka, please."

"Um ... there's no Annie Hapka working here," the girl replied.

"Did she used to work there?" Dan asked.

"Hang on, I'll ask the manager."

Within a few moments there was a more mature-sounding woman on the line. "You're looking for Ann Hapka?"

"Yes," Dan replied. "I'm an investigator from the Pine County sheriff's department, and I'm trying to find Annie Hapka."

"Ann is married now, and I'm afraid she's in the hospital."

"Which hospital?"

"Mercy Hospital, in Moose Lake. Her married name is Olsen."

Dan dialed the dispatcher and asked, "How long ago did Pam

Ryan leave this last note on my desk?"

"I don't know, Dan," she replied. "Pam signed out at about eight-thirty this morning."

Dan looked at the clock. It was nearly 11:00 a. m. "What's Pam's home phone number?"

He dialed the number and waited for five rings before a groggy Pam Ryan answered the phone.

"Pam, this is Dan."

"Oh, hi Dan," she said as the cobwebs cleared from her brain. "What's up?"

"Is Ann Olsen lucid?" he asked, "and was she able to tell you anything about her attack?"

"She slept all night. She was starting to come around a little, but I didn't really feel she was ready to answer many questions." Pam paused, then added. "I left you a note to call because she asked what I knew about Jean Oinen. I guess they knew each other."

. . .

When Dan arrived at Mercy Hospital, he thought that Ann Olsen didn't have much resemblance to the picture of the skinny little blond girl in the trailer. She looked about fifteen years older, had a little droop to her face, and probably weighed close to two-hundred pounds on a short, five-feet-four frame. She had a large patch on her head, and Dan noticed a large bruise on one side of her face.

"Mrs. Olsen, I'm Dan Williams from the Pine County sheriff's department. I'm investigating a crime that involves an old friend of yours, Jean Oinen."

"Oh, dear. I thought you were here to talk about the burglary. What happened to Jean?"

"Well, as a matter-of-fact, we're not sure, but she is missing. I'd also like to hear about your burglary, though, if you feel like talking about it."

Ann Olsen closed her eyes for a moment and pursed her lips, as if waiting for some pain to pass. Finally, she opened her eyes again and looked at Dan. "I guess it was two nights ago, now. Someone broke in and I could hear them downstairs rummaging around. I called 911, but they couldn't get a policeman to the house; they were all too far away. I heard footsteps coming up the stairs, so I loaded the shotgun and went into the baby's room. I shot at the door, but the robber got in the room, and the last thing I remember is him pulling the gun from my hand.

"Did you recognize him?" Dan asked.

"No, he was wearing a ski mask." Her voice was starting to tremble. "Tell me about Jeanie."

"There was apparently an assault in Jean's trailer a few nights ago. She hasn't been seen since."

Ann closed her eyes again. Dan waited. "She called me that night," Olsen said, without opening her eyes, "and she hasn't answered the phone since. I've tried to reach her."

"Did she ever say anything to you about her being afraid, or that something was going to happen?"

"No," Ann replied. "She *was* excited, though, the last time we talked. She said something weird, like she had figured something out and she was going to call *him*."

"Did she tell you who the man was?"

"No. She always kept it a secret. Like it was somebody very important, or something, and she didn't want people to know."

"Do you know what it was she had figured out?"

"I don't know. I hadn't seen Jean for a year or so, and then she started calling me to talk a few weeks ago. We got together a couple of times. It was great to see her again. She became very fond of Toby … our little boy. We would take little trips, you know, to Duluth, to shop for baby clothes and stuff. Then, a few days ago she called and said she had to figure out some things to get her life back together. I haven't talked to her since."

"Did you know that she's a prostitute?"

Ann smiled. "She isn't a prostitute. She entertains men, but she never charges them a cent."

"Mrs. Olsen, they pay to have sex with her."

"No way," Ann protested. "Jean enjoyed the intimacy as much as they did. She treated them special. They weren't Johns, they were friends, and they donated to keep her comfortable."

"She seems to have sold you on that pretty well."

"She believed it. I believed it, at least at first. She invited me to a few parties, and it didn't seem like anything but a party— then, anyway." A grimace crossed Ann's face as she reacted to a wave of pain.

"Are you okay? Do you need me to get the nurse?"

"I get sharp pains every now and again. I can't see straight either. There are two of you."

"Do you want me to leave?"

"No," she replied. "I'm okay. Go ahead."

"You were her partner?"

Ann smiled wanly. "I told you. She was a hostess. I went to a couple of parties she threw and had a few drinks and a few laughs."

"Do you know who her friends were?"

"I know the ones who were at the parties. My husband was one of them, until we got serious."

Williams read through the list for her. "Any that you know besides those?"

"You know about twice as many as I do. And everyone that I ever heard about is there on that list. Why are you going through this entire hassle? Why don't you just look in Jeanie's planner? Her life is in there. She didn't make a move unless it was in the planner."

"Where did she keep it?" Dan asked.

"In the desk, the one in her bedroom. Unless she went somewhere, then it was with her."

"How about her old ones. Did she save them?"

"I don't know. She may have, but I doubt it. Anyway, I never saw any."

"Tell me about Jean's father. Did you know he threw her out?"

Ann smiled again. "He caught her in bed with Mark Bergquist and just went crazy."

"You smiled when you said that. Why?"

"Well, Jean was very … um … mature for her age, both mentally and physically. She taught me more about the birds and the bees than my mom ever did. She was sexually active very early in her life, and she had the sense to realize that it was fun. That's something we small-town girls aren't ever supposed to admit."

"Can you think of anything that would make someone want to

hurt Jean?"

Ann shook her head. "No, sorry. When I talked to her last, she was very excited about this decision that she'd made. I can't imagine that it was anything bad."

"We found some blood in the trailer, and it's an unusual blood type. The medical examiner says that there is reason to believe that she must have had a transfusion at one time. Do you remember her ever being hospitalized?"

Ann shook her head again, then stopped and her mouth dropped open. "Oh, God. I'd forgotten. She ran away, when we were, like, juniors in high school. No one knows this, especially not her father. She was pregnant."

They stopped talking as a nurse came in and took Ann's blood pressure. When the nurse left, Ann went on. "Anyway, I was saying that Jean got pregnant. The baby's father gave her money to get an abortion, and she disappeared for the whole rest of the school year. She never did get back into school, and we were never close after that, until we started partying together, three or four years ago. I'll bet that she had to have been hospitalized for that. Maybe she had a transfusion then."

"Do you know where she went for the abortion?"

"She never said. But it was out of this area, like, maybe Minneapolis or St. Cloud."

"Do you know who the father was?"

"No. At the time, I assumed it was Mark Bergquist, her old boyfriend, but looking back on it I don't think so anymore."

"Who do you think it was?"

Ann considered the question before answering. "She was working as a waitress at the time. I think that she was involved with some older guy who was a customer. Mark could never have come up with the money for an abortion, and I don't think he even knew about this other person."

. . .

Williams drove back to his house. On the way, he was running through the places a girl could go to get an abortion in the middle 1980's.

Sally was warming leftover roast beef in the microwave when he walked into the kitchen. He popped the cap off a Michelob and sat down at the kitchen table.

"If you were pregnant in the mid-1980's and needed a discreet abortion, where would you go?" he asked Sally. "I had a woman tell me that her old friend went away for an abortion and she thought her friend went to St. Cloud or Minneapolis."

Sally wiped her hands on a towel and sat down. "St. Cloud was a very Catholic town and the hospital was run by nuns. That was probably not a choice. There are at least half-a-dozen clinics in the Twin Cities that provided legal abortion services, and probably another half-dozen within a four-hour drive. It could be hard to track down. And if someone wanted to be really discreet, they might go to Chicago or Las Vegas."

"Hmmm. Not the answer I wanted."

"Sorry. You asked." The buzzer went off on the microwave and Sally got up and removed the dish. "Is this a new line? Last time I can remember you were trying to figure out Orrin Petrich's connection to this sex club."

"I still am. I can tie everyone else together except him. He's dangling off the chart, out there all by himself."

"You said that someone was being less than candid with you. Is it possible that person was the link. Is he someone with political ties?"

"No," Dan replied, "he's a guy in the gravel business." Suddenly, Dan had a revelation. "The gravel business! I'll bet he sells gravel and concrete to the county and state for road projects."

Chapter 17

Williams rushed to the courthouse at 7:00 a.m. to catch Sepanen before the sheriff got into some other activities for the day. His mind had run over the Petrich-Bell connection all night and he'd had less than three hours of sleep. The sheriff was already sitting at his desk when Williams rushed in.

"John, I think that I've got the link to Petrich figured out."

The sheriff looked up from his computer with surprise. Dan almost always knocked before entering, unless he was excited.

"What is it?"

"Bell Gravel," Dan replied. "Ron Bell is the only person who's been elusive about his ties to the prostitution ring, and Petrich is the only person that I can't tie to a referral within the group. Petrich is the only one that Jean Oinen ever spoke badly about. What committees does Petrich sit on in the legislature?"

"I think that he's the chairman of something to do with allocating money."

"Would that include road construction?" Dan asked. "Like allocating funds to the people who would use gravel and concrete? Like someone that could make sure that Bell Gravel had plenty of state business?"

"There's that contract employee in the county engineer's office, uh ... Pritchard, I believe is his name ... working on right-of-way easements. Let's grab him," the sheriff said as he reached for his phone. "I think he could help us understand what's going on better."

Sepanen looked up the internal courthouse number for the county engineer's office. He punched the numbers and waited a few seconds. "Gary, this is John Sepanen. Can you pull your nose out of the plat books and come over to my office?" There was a pause. "This is very urgent. I need to see you now," the sheriff said. "Okay, you're coming right over then? ... okay ... okay, I'll see you then."

Sepanen hung up the phone. "Pritchard's on his way. Funny, but he sounded very reluctant."

While they waited, Dan updated the sheriff on the Oinen investigation and the possible link to Ann Olsen's attack.

The knock on the door interrupted them. They looked up and saw the county engineer's contract employee, Gary Pritchard, looking like he'd lost his last friend. The thirty-year-old looked gray and tired.

"Gary," the sheriff said, "grab a chair."

Pritchard pulled up a chair and sat with it turned so he was facing Williams.

"Gary," Dan asked, "what committee is Orrin Petrich on?"

Pritchard frowned. "He's the chairman of the transportation committee. Why?"

"Which committee identifies the state road projects and allocates the funds?"

"The transportation committee."

"Do you know how many state contracts Bell Gravel has?"

Pritchard's expression grew grim. "Look. I think I don't want to answer any more of these questions until I see a lawyer."

Williams and Sepanen stared at each other in disbelief. Sepanen pushed his phone slowly across the desk toward Pritchard. "Go ahead."

Pritchard reached for the phone then pulled his hand back. "I think this needs to be a private conversation. I think I'll call from my office."

He started to rise from the chair, when Williams put his hand on the engineer's shoulder.

"Sit down, Gary. We don't know exactly what's going on here, but I think you'd better not make any calls to anyone other than a lawyer right now."

Gary looked at the sheriff. "I'll call my lawyer."

. . .

Half an hour later they were sitting in the sheriff's office with Tom Parrish, the assistant county attorney, and Roger Appledorn, the attorney Pritchard had summoned.

Parrish asked to be briefed on the situation, and Williams spent several minutes explaining his speculation about the Petrich-Bell connection to Appledorn and Parrish while Pritchard squirmed.

"So," Parrish summarized, looking at John Sepanen, "you called Gary in here to try and understand the process of allo-cating the state road projects, and he asked to have Roger present?"

The sheriff nodded. The county attorney turned to Pritchard and asked, "Guilty conscience?"

There was no reply.

"How hard is it for a civil engineer to get a job if he's been caught with his hand in the till, Gary?" Parrish asked, looking directly at Pritchard. Pritchard looked away. "I'd guess that it's pretty tough," the county attorney continued. He turned his attention to Roger Appledorn. "Let's play out a scenario here: We talk through this thing with Bell Gravel and try to figure out how it ties to the Oinen case. Your client lays all his cards on the table, we accept a resignation from him, assuming he repays any money that went into his pocket. He testifies for the state in any proceedings, assuming there are no violent felonies involved on his part."

Appledorn turned to Pritchard. "Let me talk to Gary privately for a moment. May we use your office, Dan?"

"Sure," said Dan. He pulled his chair back and let Pritchard and Appledorn out the door. In less than five minutes, they were back.

"We want the agreement in writing," Appledorn said. "No charges against Gary for anything related to Bell Gravel or Petrich. In return, Gary gives his complete cooperation."

The lawyers left for the county attorney's office to draft the agreement, and in half an hour the five men were back in Sepanen's office. Appledorn nodded to his client, who looked nervously at Williams and Sepanen.

"What do you want to know?" Pritchard asked.

Williams pressed the record button on a cassette tape player and pushed it toward Pritchard. "What's the tie between Orrin Petrich and Bell Gravel?"

Pritchard cleared his throat. "Petrich gets the State Department of Transportation to spend money up here. He feeds Bell bidding information and Bell wins every bid. Bell passes cash back to Petrich."

"What are you so nervous about" Dan asked, "other than the fact that you knew about a felony kickback scheme and didn't report it?"

"Well," Pritchard said, "Bell supplies substandard concrete and class five gravel. It's cheaper for him. That's how he can afford to be the low bidder and still pay off Petrich."

"Do you know how Petrich and Bell are tied to the Oinen case?" Dan asked.

Pritchard shifted in his chair and looked at the doorway for salvation. None arrived. "Not entirely," he replied nervously. "Bell asked me to find a diary or appointment book in Dan's office. I only found a list of names, but I passed it along to Bell. I know he's scared to death of something that he thinks is in that appointment book."

"But you don't know what that is?" the sheriff asked.

"No."

"Do you know how much money changes hands between Bell and Petrich?"

Pritchard shook his head.

"Do you know how the money is passed?"

Again Pritchard shook his head, but after a moment he said, "Well, not entirely, anyway. I think it has something to do with the hooker in the trailer."

Dan and John Sepanen glanced at one another knowingly. "They were passing the money at Jean Oinen's trailer?" asked Dan.

"I think that might be it," said Pritchard.

"How long has this been going on?" Dan asked.

"About two-and-a-half years," Pritchard replied. "Since the big project that started to resurface the interstate."

Williams snapped his fingers. "Like twenty-nine months?" he asked.

"I guess about that."

Williams looked at the sheriff. Sepanen reached over and pressed the pause button on the recorder.

"We recovered an envelope from the victim's trailer with the number twenty-nine written on the corner, John," said Williams to Sepanen. "It had three-thousand dollars in cash inside."

"But Petrich was at the Oinen trailer the night of the incident," Sepanen said. "Why was the money still there?"

"Good question. Maybe he was too excited after he murdered Jean Oinen to remember to pick it up."

"Maybe," said the sheriff. "Tom, have we got enough to arrest Ron Bell?" Sepanen asked of the county attorney.

"I'd like to get a search warrant to seize his financial records and shipping records at the same time," Parrish said. He turned to the engineer. "What else do we need to prove that he was supplying substandard materials?"

"Well, you'll need the mix records from the concrete plant to prove what they were making for the roadway. Then you'd need all the trucking records to show which pre-mixed batches went to which of his work sites. I suppose you could look at which gravel pit they used for which project. Some of the pits are higher grade material than others."

"In short," Parrish summarized, looking at Dan and Sepanen, "we'll need everything."

"I'd like to keep the scope of this limited to Bell Gravel for the time being," the sheriff said. "Let's let Petrich think he's clear for a while until I can tie some of these other things together."

"You don't want to flush him out now?" Parrish asked.

"Not yet. We can go for half the stuff now, or wait a little and then take him down for taking bribes as well as murder."

. . .

Williams popped two Tums in his mouth on the way to his desk. On the message spike was a pink slip that said simply, "Call Laurie."

He dialed the number for the Minnesota Bureau of Criminal Apprehension in St. Paul. Laurie Lone Eagle picked up the phone on the first ring.

"You left a very brief message," said Dan.

"Hi, Dan. That's because I don't know, never knew, and will swear that I never told you the information that you are about to hear," Laurie said. "The Minnesota State Attorney General is going to take over the Oinen case." Her voice was almost a whisper.

"What!" exclaimed Dan. "Did I hear you right?"

"You heard it."

"What the hell … do you know why?"

"I'm not entirely clear on it. I assume Petrich is involved and has put pressure on the AG to take it over and bury it."

"But why would the attorney general agree to something like that?"

"Petrich has something on a lot of people here. I assume that the AG is no different."

"Are you serious? He has something on the attorney general?"

"Oh, Dan," Laurie said, "you are so naive. Haven't you ever heard of Huey Long, John Daley or J. Edgar Hoover? That's how those men consolidated their power. Petrich is not above anything that will preserve his influence."

"Shit!" Dan uttered. "We may be within a day or two of nailing him."

"For the murder?"

"At least for accepting bribes and rigging the bidding on road construction projects."

"No shit? You've got hard evidence?"

"We're going to execute a search warrant on his co-conspirator within the hour." Dan replied.

"All right! Nail him to a cross."

"Yeah, but that's only half the loaf," Dan said. "I think he's in on the murder, too. I want to nail him on everything. Is there anyway you can slow things down with the attorney general from there?"

"Get serious," Laurie said. "I'm a peon in the BCA. You're talking about influencing the head law enforcement man in the State of Minnesota."

"What can he do if we have a pat case?" Dan asked.

"He could plea bargain it to a petty misdemeanor and bury it without an investigation," Laurie replied. "He could not bother to investigate any of the other potential crimes involved. He could even decide that you hicks had screwed up the evidence somehow and throw it all out."

"Say, what do you know about Petrich's aide, Tom Hansen?"

"I've never checked for a record, if that's what you mean. I do know that they are inseparable."

"Check it out," Dan suggested. "If you would be so kind."

"Return the favor some day," Laurie said with a sigh.

Williams hung up and looked at the receiver glumly. He was still staring at the phone when the sheriff stuck his head around the doorframe.

"The show's ready to roll. Are you coming?"

Dan was roused from his trance. "What?"

"We've got the search warrant. Are you coming along?"

"Wouldn't miss it."

On the way out the door, Dan popped two more Tums in his mouth.

. . .

The caravan pulled up to the trailer at the gravel pit. Two marked squads led the way, followed by Sepanen and Williams in Dan's unmarked car, and the assistant county attorney with two investigators in the final car.

Inside the trailer, the scene was comical. The man Williams had seen sitting at the computer on his last visit was there when the county attorney came in. Tom Parrish handed him the search warrant. By the time Williams got into the limited space inside the trailer, the man was talking frantically with Ron Bell on the cell phone, begging for direction.

The two investigators were directing the deputies to file cabinets of records. They started loading files into boxes over the protests of the man behind the counter.

The sound of crunching gravel outside announced the arrival of Ron Bell. He raced up the steps of the trailer and came to a stop just inside the door.

"What the hell is going on?" Bell asked.

Williams turned toward the new arrival. "Well, Ron, it seems we have evidence that you've been cheating the county and state on gravel and concrete. We're seizing all your records as evidence."

"Get the hell out of here," Bell shouted. "You have no right to my records."

The county attorney rose from where he had been searching the computer files. He handed Bell the search warrant. "This says we have the right."

"This is bullshit. I'm calling my lawyer."

Bell moved toward the phone and Williams laid a hand on his arm. "You can call from the jail."

Bell ripped his arm from Williams' grip and then threw a punch with the opposite fist. Williams deflected the punch using Bell's momentum to spin him around and push him face first into the wall. He twisted Bell's arm into a hammerlock behind his back and held it tight.

"Assaulting an officer is a felony, Ron. Shouldn't do that. We'll have to search and cuff you now." He placed the other hand wide on the wall and pushed the left foot wide while he ran his hands over Bell's body, searching for a weapon. Bell protested, but Dan ignored him.

Williams pulled a pair of handcuffs from his belt and pulled Bell's hands down one at a time and latched them into the cuffs.

"You're under arrest. You have the right to … "

. . .

At the courthouse, Gary Pritchard was assisting the attorneys with interpretation of the data they had gathered from the trailer. Dan watched an attorney work his way through the computerized files. He grew uneasy over the slow progress and was popping more Tums when the dispatcher paged him. He picked up the phone and punched the flashing button.

"Williams."

"Dan, Oresek here. I think we have your missing woman."

"Jean Oinen?" Dan asked.

"We won't know for sure until we get some dental records or get an ID from a relative. But the wounds are right and the age is right."

"Where are you?"

"I'm calling from a cell phone," Oresek said. "I'm parked in a Carlton County park at the Barnum exit on I-35. A couple of fishermen found a woman's body on the island in Bear Lake this afternoon, when they stopped off for a bathroom break."

"It's been pretty cool. How bad is the decomposition?"

"That's really weird," Oresek said. "She's thawing out. There's no decomposition evident."

There was a long pause. "Thawing out, as in frozen?" Dan

asked. "It hasn't been that cold."

"Tell you what. We're taking her to Duluth. Can you find someone to ID the body?"

Dan thought for a second, then said, "The father lives in Moose Lake. I can try to catch him, or there's an old friend who lives there, too. I'll get one of them and meet you at the morgue."

Chapter 18

Dan Williams called Elmer Oinen's trailer and got an answer on the third ring. It sounded like he was eating. Williams checked his watch; it was 5:15 p.m.

"Mr. Oinen," Dan said. "I'm sorry to interrupt your supper, and I'm sorry to have to break this kind of news to you, but I got a call from the medical examiner in Duluth. They found a body and they believe it's Jean."

There was a long pause. "Are they sure?" Oinen asked.

"They need you to make an identification. Could you meet me at the Miller Dwan hospital morgue?"

Again there was a long pause. "Is there some other way to do this? Can't they do one of those genetic tests?"

"I'm sorry," Dan said. "I know this is a shock, and it's very difficult, but this is the fastest and surest way they have."

"When do you want me there?"

"As soon as you can get there. I'll be leaving Pine City in a few minutes."

"Does she look okay?" Oinen asked hesitantly. "I mean, will I be able to tell it's her?"

"I think so. The coroner asked me to bring someone to make the identification. If there is some question about being able to make the identification visually, they usually try to do it through dental records."

"Oh, ... Okay. I'll be there."

. . .

Williams called Sally and warned her not to hold supper. It was apparently something she had already ascertained.

"A big breakthrough?" she asked.

"They found Jean Oinen's body in Barnum today. I'm headed for Duluth now."

"Anything that points to Petrich?"

"We've got some motive," Dan said, "but no physical evidence at this point."

At the hospital, Williams parked in a spot marked for police vehicles. It was near the morgue door the morticians used to pick up bodies. Inside, he found the medical examiner's assistant, Eddie Paulson, sitting at a desk reading through some reports. His ponytail of salt-and-pepper hair seemed out of place in the morgue.

"Hi, Dan." The rehabilitated Vietnam veteran shook his hand. Williams thought back to the grumpy, shell of a man Eddie had been before the medical examiner had rescued him from the vet's hospital.

"Any sign of Elmer Oinen?" Dan asked.

"Not yet. We probably still need him to make the visual, but this body matches the blood type in the trailer. B-positive, with

Kell antibodies. Probably not two other people in the state with that combination."

"Any other preliminary findings?"

"One deep wound on the neck. It probably went into the carotid artery. No other significant trauma to the body that we saw."

"Tony said she was frozen."

"Weirdest thing," Eddie said, shaking his head, "most bodies that sit outside this time of year are, but not to this extent. I went to take a rectal temperature and couldn't insert the thermometer. I probed with a gloved finger and came back with ice crystals. She was frozen solid, except for a little surface thawing."

"Why would someone freeze a corpse?" Dan asked.

"There are some real fruitcakes out there, Dan, as you well know," Eddie said. "Maybe it was some guy that wanted her for later. And then there's that bunch that freezes corpses and hopes to revive them at some time in the future when the medical practice improves."

The door opened behind them and a very apprehensive Elmer Oinen walked in.

"Mr. Oinen." Williams offered his hand. "I'm awfully sorry to put you through this. This is Eddie Paulson, the medical examiner's assistant."

Oinen merely nodded to Paulson, who said "Please follow me," and then led them into a room with a wall lined by large refrigerator doors. He checked the tag on one and opened it. Inside was a gurney cart with a black body bag.

Eddie pulled the gurney out of the vault and unzipped the body bag about eighteen inches. He spread the black plastic, exposing a waxy female face, surrounded by blood-encrusted brown hair that had matted against the skin.

Williams took a quick look at the woman's face, then watched Elmer Oinen. Tears started to form in the corners of his eyes and his mouth opened. Then, Oinen started to shake and sob and Williams tried to catch him as he fell to his knees. Deep, croaking sobs came in waves as Williams helped him back to his feet and to a chair.

Eddie zipped the bag shut, rolled the gurney back into the vault, and closed the door with a thump that resonated through the tiled room.

After a few minutes, Elmer composed himself and looked at Williams, his eyes red and full of grief. "Now what do I do?" he said, as if it were a question he had held for a long time as far as Jeanie was concerned.

Dan studied Oinen's face. "Are you Okay, Mr. Oinen?

"Yeah. Yeah. I'm Okay. What's next?"

"Well, you'll have to call a funeral director," said Dan, "and make arrangements to have her picked up. They'll contact Eddie and do the rest."

Eddie walked up with a form on a clipboard and indicated a line for Oinen to sign. Elmer signed shakily, then rose and walked out.

Dan and Eddie looked at one another and Eddie just shook his head. "That's always tough," he said.

"When's Tony going to do the post postmortem?" Dan asked.

"First thing in the morning. We just wrapped one up and he's dictating notes. You could go in and talk to him, if you wanted."

"No," Dan replied. "I've got some more things to get done yet tonight. I'll see you in the morning, if I can get away."

. . .

On the drive back to Pine City, Williams was reviewing several scenarios. It was nearly eight o'clock when he walked past the dispatcher, enclosed in her chamber of bulletproof glass, and nearly ran into Sandy Maki.

"Dan! I've been hoping you'd come back." Sandy had just come in for his night patrol shift a little before Dan had arrived.

"What's up?"

"You had supper yet?"

"I just did. Two of them, and they're calcium rich. The commercials say so."

"You ought to see a doctor," Maki said. "Something's eating your insides. I got some fingerprint results for you."

Williams motioned for Sandy to follow him and they walked to William's office and sat down. Williams pulled two more Tums from his pocket and popped them into his mouth. "It's this job that's eating my guts," he said. "What did you get on the fingerprints?"

"You were right about checking the clean dishes and glasses. They were loaded with prints. That's the good news. The bad news is, we didn't get matches except for a few." Maki shuffled through some papers until he found the one he wanted. "We got three matches from the NCIC computer: Harold Nord, the teacher from Moose Lake; Patrick Rooney, the insurance man from Willow River, and ... " he strung out the drama, "Orrin Petrich, your close personal friend."

"I'll be damned!" Dan said. "They *all* had criminal records?"

"No. These came up from old military records. I got Ron Bell's prints from booking," Maki added. "He also matches."

"Did you match any prints from the blood on the bathtub and floor?" Dan asked.

"Most were smears. I think the one set we got in the bedroom was from the victim."

"You can check that with the ME in Duluth," Dan said. "They found the body today."

"Oh, yeah? I hadn't heard that. Where'd they find her?"

"The island in Bear Lake."

Maki whistled. "That's a long way from Sturgeon Lake. She didn't float there."

Williams cracked his first smile in many hours. "The weird part is, she was frozen solid. Couldn't have been there too long."

"Frozen solid? How'd that happen? It's not *that* cold."

"Only thing I can figure out is someone put her in a deep freeze, or something."

"My God," said Maki, "what a world."

"You got it, Sandy, my boy. You got it. You heard the latest on Bell Gravel?"

"Sheriff filled me in. You think Petrich murdered that girl?"

"Looks like he had the motive, the means and the opportunity, " said Dan, smiling.

"Oh," Maki said, "that reminds me. When Pam and I were going over the trailer, we kept getting these smears that looked like fingerprints, but we couldn't find any ridges. They looked like a glove print." Maki fumbled through more reports. "So I pulled one with tape and sent it, along with some residue that I found around the edge of the bathtub, to the BCA, in St. Paul."

Maki pulled out the report and handed it to Williams. "It was cornstarch. Like they use on surgical gloves."

"Hmm. The doctor-link again. That goes against Petrich … unless he had medical training somewhere in his smoky past," Dan said. "The ME says the cut was very specific, into the artery in the neck. Maybe we should be looking for a surgeon, or someone who works in a hospital."

"Well," Maki replied, "the BCA says that the gloves are available through any pharmacy. So from that angle it wouldn't have to be a medical person. But the skill involved certainly points that way." Maki was more or less talking to himself now. "But it is an interesting twist. I'd say this wasn't a second-degree crime. Someone came with surgical gloves in their pocket."

Williams leaned back in his chair and smiled. "Good work, Sandy. I mean it. That's good work. Now, do you think we should go and arrest Orrin Petrich immediately, or later?"

Maki smiled. "Hey! Just give me a little more time, Dan."

. . .

After Maki left, Williams sat at his desk for a few minutes mulling over the day's events, attempting to sort out the angles. He was just about to leave when another possibility occurred to him. He dialed the number in the phone book for the Minnesota state capitol. A recording came on, giving him information about tours.

He tapped his pencil on the desktop for a few seconds then

called information in St. Paul. He requested the phone number for Thomas Hansen, spelling the name out. There were eight listed, and he didn't have a clue where Orrin Petrich's aide might live.

He called a private number for State Capitol Security.

"This is Dan Williams, undersheriff for Pine County. I'm in the midst of an investigation and I need to get in touch with Tom Hansen, Orrin Petrich's aide." He disliked using his title, but he hoped it would give some clout with the receptionist on duty.

"I'll have to check a couple of directories, Sheriff Williams. Please give me a number where I can reach you in the next few minutes."

He gave the receptionist the number for the county dispatcher and waited by the phone. It was reassuring that capitol security didn't hand out the private phone numbers of staff over the phone to anyone claiming to be in law enforcement. It had become common practice that a recall be made to verify the identity of persons making incoming calls. Media people, claiming they were someone else before caller ID became available, had burned too many receptionists.

A light blinked on his phone and the dispatcher's voice came over the intercom, paging him. "Williams here."

"Sheriff, Mister Hansen is out of the office, but his home number is ..."

Williams dialed the St. Paul number. The prefix indicated that it was downtown, and Williams had a vision of Hansen running to the phone in one of the condominiums, high on the St. Paul skyline.

"Hello." The voice sounded sleepy and Williams realized that it was nearly nine-thirty.

"Tom Hansen?"

"Yes."

"This is Dan Williams, undersheriff of Pine County. Sorry to bother you, but I need to ask you a couple of questions. I understand that you drive Senator Petrich everywhere he goes. Is that correct?"

Hansen pondered the question. There was nothing incriminating in the question itself. "That's right."

"Can you tell me where you and the senator were last Tuesday evening?"

Hansen rolled his eyes. He quickly remembered Tuesday as the night of the trip to Sturgeon Lake. "Not off the top of my head," he lied.

"Could you please look it up?" Williams asked.

Hansen grew wary. "I don't think so. Why do you want to know?"

"I'm investigating a murder in Sturgeon Lake and I thought that either you or the senator may have been an unknowing witness at the scene."

"I'm sorry, Sheriff Williams, but we were at … a reception for the Democratic leadership, in St. Cloud." Although he had hesitated briefly, the lie sounded credible to Hansen.

"Would you please check your calendar and verify that?" Dan asked.

"Sure. Just a second." Hansen went into the bedroom and pulled out his calendar. It showed he and Petrich had gone to St. Cloud on Monday evening for a Democratic fund raiser. Pretty light turnout in that land of the John Birch Society, he thought. Nobody would probably remember which night it was held anyway.

"Williams? I just checked my calendar. We were in St. Cloud that whole evening."

"And," Dan asked, "you're sure that was Tuesday night?"

"Right," Hansen replied emphatically. "That was Tuesday."

"Well, thanks, Tom. That helps clear some things up."

"No problem. Always happy to assist." Hansen hung up the phone. "Stupid bastard. He deserves to be stuck in Pine County," he said to himself.

. . .

Dan drove home, showered and climbed into bed.

"You're late tonight," Sally said as she rolled over and pecked Dan on the cheek.

"Yeah. We've got a lot of things going on, and a deadline."

"A deadline?" she asked.

"Laurie Lone Eagle said the grapevine has the Minnesota attorney general going to take over the Oinen investigation."

"What for? It isn't that high profile, is it?"

"Apparently Senator Petrich is scared to death and he wants it where he can control it. Laurie says that Petrich has something on the AG."

"They play hard poker don't they?"

"Yeah," Dan said, "but I've got a few trump cards they don't know about."

Chapter 19

Williams was in the sheriff's office at seven the next morning to leave a note about finding Jean Oinen's body. He stopped off at his desk and pulled out the card for William Peikert's office in Hinckley. He expected to leave a message, but the old lawyer answered his own phone.

"Mr. Peikert, Jean Oinen's body was located yesterday, and her father made a positive identification. The medical examiner is doing a post postmortem this morning." Dan paused to let the news sink in. "Can you tell me who Jean Oinen was looking for?"

There was a pause. "You have a *positive* identification of the body?" Piekert asked.

"From her father."

"Then, I guess there is no reason to keep it quiet anymore. Miss Oinen had a child, in 1987. She asked me to locate the baby and the adoptive parents. The little girl is fourteen years old now."

"Have you made any progress?' Dan asked.

"I've traded letters with the adoption agency in Willmar,

Minnesota. But, so far I haven't received any hard information."

"I have a search warrant for the safe-deposit box," Dan said. "Will you fight it?"

"I don't see any point anymore."

"I'm going to try and wrap up a few things on another aspect of the case today. I'm going to the bank tomorrow morning. Would you like to join me as a witness?"

"I think that would be appropriate," Peikert replied. "Let me clear the calendar. Shall we say nine o-clock?"

. . .

Dan drove to Duluth and found the Hospital's parking spot for police vehicles taken. He drove around for five minutes before finding an open spot in the visitor's lot to park. By the time he got to the hospital morgue it was 9:25 a.m.

Eddie Paulson and Dr. Tony Oresek had begun the post post-mortem when Dan walked into the autopsy room. The nude, female body was lying on a stainless steel-table as Oresek and Paulson, dressed in blue, surgical-scrub clothing, worked their way around the periphery of the table. Oresek's gloved hands prodded and touched the skin as he made comments into a microphone that hung over the table. Paulson was using a microscope to find and remove hairs and fibers from the body. The sweet odor of disinfectant overpowered the odor of death. But that would last only until Oresek opened the abdomen.

"Come here, Dan," Oresek said. "There's a big bruise here, in the hair behind the ear. It was probably enough to knock her unconscious." Oresek spread a bloody patch of hair to reveal the discolored lump on the skin. The bloody hair discolored his surgical gloves.

Williams bent over the body and saw the raised knot with the skin broken.

Oresek moved to the side of the table and spread the skin of the woman's neck with two fingers. "The neck wound is actually very small." He exposed a deep gash that was only two inches long. There was no blood evident on the neck at all. "I'd say this was a real professional job," Oresek observed. "Most killers tend to overdo the cut because they don't know anatomy. They leave the corpse looking like a PEZ dispenser. Whoever did this was very specific. They cut through to the carotid artery and no more. Quick, precise and deadly."

"So, I should be looking for an MD?" Dan asked.

"That would be one possibility. The other might be a butcher or a professional killer. Professional hit men usually go for the heart or the spine, leaving little or no external bleeding. This was pretty messy. Professionals don't like to get their hands dirty. Whoever did this wasn't much concerned about leaving a mess."

"The killer was a *little* concerned," Dan observed, "he moved her to the bathtub before he slit her throat. He knew there would be a lot of blood."

Oresek went back to his minute search of the surface of the body. "No evidence of needle marks. She wasn't drugged. Very fine scars under the areolas from an apparent breast augmentation."

Oresek paused over the abdomen. "Interesting mid-line mark. She must have had a child sometime." He pushed the legs wide and spread the pubic hair. "Episiotomy scar, too. No evidence of forced penetration or other surface trauma."

Oresek stepped back from the table as Eddie pulled a cart over beside it. Oresek peeled back the blue surgical towel covering the cart and revealed an array of knives, saws, and other items that looked like they belonged in a torture chamber. He selected a long knife and made an incision from the pubis to the navel. Above the navel he made two more incisions reaching to the armpits, forming a "Y." The odor of cadaverine filled the room and overpowered the disinfectant. He peeled back the skin and started to push around the internal organs, making comments into the microphone about the condition of each.

"She must have been a drinker," Oresek noted. "The liver looks fatty for someone this young. No recent evidence of a meal in the stomach."

He took out another, smaller knife, and made a cut inside the abdomen, near the pubis.

"Get a vial, Eddie."

Oresek collected some fluid and handed the vial back to his assistant. "Mark it 'vaginal sample A'."

"I thought you said she was a prostitute, Dan?" Oresek asked.

"That's what all her customers said."

"I've never seen a professional with semen in her vagina, unless they'd been raped. Call girls are generally very careful and make their Johns wear condoms. If she was a working girl, there should have been a supply of condoms near the bed somewhere, and maybe a few used ones in a wastebasket. Did your investigators find any?"

"Pam Ryan made the same observation," Dan said, "She

questioned why a prostitute wouldn't have a supply of condoms in her bedroom."

Oresek reached back into the body and felt around the lower abdomen. "Her fallopian tubes are in pretty bad shape. There appears to be some scarring. I wonder if she'd had an infection that wasn't treated quickly and it left her sterile? That could be part of the reason she didn't use condoms, if she wasn't worried about a pregnancy."

"There was an outbreak of gonorrhea among her clients," Dan said. "Could that have caused the scarring?"

"Could be," Oresek said. "I would have thought someone in a close-knit group would have been diagnosed quickly and treatment would be effective before this much damage would've been done, though. Of course, who's to say the recent infection was the only one she's had. If she's been sexually active with many partners, she's been at high risk for a lot of nasty infections."

After taking a few organ samples, Oresek moved to the top of the table. He made a cut along the back of the hairline and pulled the scalp forward over the face. He used an air-powered Stryker saw to cut through the cranium, then he delicately removed the skullcap.

"Big hematoma here, in the left occipital region. Corresponds with the lump behind the ear. I would say she was probably unconscious when her throat was cut."

Williams saw a pink lump with a rusty area where Oresek was pointing. "That would correspond with the interrupted scream the neighbor heard," he said. "Any speculation on the instrument?"

Oresek turned the skullcap in his hand and then went back to the brain. "Cracked her pretty hard … a sharp break line. I'm assuming it will correspond with the hairs we found on the head of the bed."

The rest of the post postmortem was uneventful. Oresek finished up his inspection and pulled off the rubber gloves.

"Pretty girl." He shook his head. "I'll try to get the full report to you tomorrow."

. . .

Williams drove back to Pine City with a hundred thoughts going through his head. Too many things to do and too little time, he thought, same as always. In his office he made a few phone calls and located the chairman of the St. Cloud Democratic Party. The man was almost too friendly in his greeting, and Dan could tell that a job like chairman of a political party chapter suited him just fine.

"I understand that Senator Petrich and his aide, Tom Hansen, were there for a fund-raiser last week. Can you verify that, sir?" Williams asked.

"Oh, yes. Certainly. The senator was our keynote speaker. A very good speech, as I recall. Senator Petrich is helping us push through some legislation for development in St. Cloud, you know."

"That so? That's pretty exciting stuff for a Tuesday night," said Williams.

"It *is* very exciting, yes … but … Tuesday night, you say? Let me see, now. Yes, I'm sure it was Monday night, not Tuesday. I remember because we were afraid there might not be as big a turn out as we'd hoped, it being a Monday night."

"You wouldn't get me out on a Monday night for a speech, Mr. Chairman, that's for sure."

The man laughed. "Oh, I doubt that, Sheriff Williams. I doubt that."

"Well, thank you, sir. You've been a big help."

When Dan hung up, a light was blinking on the phone. One of the jailers walked in and told him there was a call on hold.

"Williams."

"Hi, Dan." Laurie Lone Eagle's voice sounded tired. "I got some information about Tom Hansen."

"Great." Dan said as he scrambled for a pencil. "What have you got?"

"Well, first, he was a student at Carleton College, in Northfield. He got arrested once for demonstrating at an abortion clinic in St. Paul. That was apparently no big deal, since he returned to Carleton. But he was busted in Northfield for possession of a controlled substance. There's not a lot in the file, but I talked to the arresting officer and it was plea bargained down from intent, to distribute, to simple possession." She let that dangle, for a moment.

"Uh, huh ... " said Dan, writing as fast as he could.

"The arresting officer wasn't pleased," Lone Eagle continued. "Hansen had a sealed record as a minor in Albert Lea, where he went to high school. It seems that the Albert Lea Police had a good memory and Northfield wasn't his first drug bust; but because he was under eighteen at the time of his first arrest, his file had been sealed by law. The Northfield police leaked that information to the dean of students at Carleton, and they threw him out. He finished his bachelor's degree, in political science, at the University of Minnesota, in Minneapolis."

"Uh huh … " said Dan, finishing his writing. "Great work Laurie. Can you FAX me the files?"

"Sure, Dan." She sounded very tired. "But you have to work quick. The state attorney general has a meeting with Sheriff Sepanen this afternoon."

Williams froze. "With Sepanen? Where?"

"The AG's office, in the State Capitol building."

"Do you know what time?" Dan asked.

"I thought that I was doing pretty well to have this much," Laurie said defensively.

"Hey. If you don't ask for the stars, you never get any."

Laurie laughed, some of the tiredness draining from her voice. "Go get'em Dan. But watch your backside. These politicians have big teeth and they bite hard."

"Right, but I got a tough backside, Laurie. You take care."

. . .

Williams walked down the hall to the sheriff's office. The sheriff was on the phone and looked very concerned. He motioned to the chair and Williams sat down.

Sepanen hung up the phone and looked at Williams somberly. " Where are you with the Oinen investigation?"

"We know she was a prostitute and that she was killed by a single stab wound to the neck. I've got stacks of money and an envelope that was probably left for Petrich. I've got a sealed safe-deposit box that I hope contains some records that will point to a killer. I've got Petrich's aide, a former drug dealer, lying to me about where Petrich was the night of the murder. That's about it."

"That was the Minnesota state attorney general, himself, on the phone. I have a command performance at three, this afternoon. He wants an update on the Oinen case."

"Correction, John," Dan said. "The AG wants to formally pull the case from us and bury it before we nail Petrich on something. Don't ask me how I know."

Sepanen's eyebrows raised quizzically, then he grinned. "So, have you got a plan?" He asked. "We can nail Petrich on the bribery charge. Do we grab that, or use it as a negotiating point?"

"Let me make two phone calls," Dan said, "and then I'll go home and change into my best white uniform shirt. Then I'll ride with you to the capitol. I'll call capitol security and have someone ready to escort us at two o'clock."

"But we don't meet the AG until three."

"I know," Dan said.

. . .

At 1:55 p.m., Williams and Sepanen pulled up in front of the capitol and met an officer in a state patrol uniform. He directed them to a parking spot.

"I'm Cory Jesperson," the officer said, introducing himself. "Please, come this way."

They walked up the steps of the capitol building and into the rotunda. They stopped to let a group of school children walk past.

Jesperson pointed to a tattered flag protected by security glass. "Do you know what this is?" he asked.

Dan and the sheriff shook their heads.

"It's the battle flag the First Minnesota Company carried when they repulsed the Confederate charge at Gettysburg," Jesperson explained. "Over eighty percent of the company was killed or wounded. It brings tears to my eyes every time I think about it."

They quietly read the plaque mounted on the window. "Cory," Dan said, breaking the silence, "we're going to arrest Tom Hansen, Senator Petrich's aide, for obstruction of justice and rendering false statements to a law enforcement officer. What's the protocol?"

"Whew! That's heavy stuff," said Jesperson. "I'd better get the sergeant-at-arms of the senate to go with us."

"Let's do it," the sheriff said.

. . .

The sergeant-at-arms was in his office and Sepanen explained their plan. The sergeant led them to Petrich's office. In the ante-room, the receptionist informed them that Mr. Hansen was "in conference" with the senator. Williams knocked on the door.

"What?" came the gruff response from within.

Williams opened the door and walked in with Sepanen at his heels.

"Senator Petrich, Mr. Hansen. I'm Undersheriff Williams and

this is Sheriff Sepanen, from Pine County. We're here to arrest Mr. Hansen."

Petrich's face went blank, then he nearly flew out of his chair. "What the hell kind of bullshit is this? Get out of here before I have you thrown out!"

Hansen sat in the chair with his mouth gaping as Petrich came around the desk and confronted Williams. "You heard me. I told you to get out."

Williams reached inside his coat and pulled out a piece of paper. "I have a felony arrest warrant for Thomas Hansen, Senator. I intend to take him into custody."

"This is the State Capitol," Petrich huffed. "You can't pull your petty bullshit here. Get out before I call security and have you thrown out."

Cory Jesperson peeked around the corner. "Sorry, Senator. It's a legal arrest warrant. They can serve it."

Hansen was out of his chair. "What are you arresting me for? I haven't done anything. You can't arrest me."

"You *are* under arrest, Mr. Hansen; for making false statements to a law enforcement officer and obstructing a police investigation, both felonies. They should be worth about five years in Stillwater, with your past record for drug use."

Petrich pushed past them and out the door. "Laura … Laura, call the sergeant at … ." Petrich stopped when he saw the sergeant at arms standing next to the receptionist's desk. "Throw them out, Roger!"

"I can't, Senator. It's legal."

"Bullshit! Get the attorney general on the phone." Petrich directed his comments at the receptionist, who began to fumble with the phone. When Petrich came back in his office, Dan was putting handcuffs on Hansen.

"Let me go," Hansen demanded. "I haven't done anything."

"You lied to me about where you were last Tuesday night. That's obstruction of a murder investigation. You're in deep trouble. We know that you and the senator were at Sturgeon Lake the night of the murder. We have witnesses that he was there to pick up his monthly payment from the gravel company."

"Yes!" Hansen yelled, suddenly. "Yes. He was there. I waited in the car. I had nothing to do with any murder."

Petrich was red with rage and lunged toward the sobbing Hansen. "Shut up, you fool!" he yelled, bowling Hansen over. Cory Jesperson grabbed Petrich from behind and tried to hold him off the handcuffed Hansen. Petrich ranted on. "Shut up or I'll have you castrated!"

Sepanen and Williams lifted Hansen from the floor. A trickle of blood ran down from Hansen's hairline. He continued to blurt out his story. "He was mad," he said, looking directly at the senator. "The hooker threw him out. He threatened to kill her."

Petrich broke free and lunged at Hansen again. "Shut up, you stupid fool!"

Williams deflected Petrich into the desk, pulling one arm behind Petrich's back.

"Okay, Senator. You're interfering with an arrest. I suggest you let your aide make his statement, or we'll have to arrest you, too." Dan was twisting the senator's arm who was grimacing in pain. He just stood there, glaring at Hansen.

Hansen was standing with a look of shock, as his mentor was being held. After a second, he found his tongue and faced Petrich defiantly. "He was so mad he forgot to pick up the bribe money. We got to Forest Lake and he made me turn around and go back."

"Did he go in and get the money then?" Dan asked, holding on to Petrich tighter. The senator was so angry his face was red and he was almost sputtering.

"No," said Hansen. "He wanted me to go to the door. But an old man was walking around in the courtyard with his dog. Then we heard sirens coming, so I just drove past and we left without the money."

Dan gave the sheriff a look of disappointment. The sheriff asked Hansen, "How often did you go to the trailer to pick up money?"

"It was a monthly payment," Hansen explained. "We've been doing it for over two years now. It's the gravel company's pay-off for getting them sealed bid information. The senator gets three thousand a month ... cash."

"Does he get any other pay-offs?" Dan asked.

"From St. Peter and Grand Rapids."

"I have the attorney general on line two, Senator," the receptionist announced over the intercom.

Williams reached over and picked up the phone. "The senator is busy right now." He hung up the receiver.

Petrich rubbed his shoulder and glared at Hansen. "You damned fool! You had the gravy train to the top and you threw it away."

He shifted his gaze to Sepanen. "And you are a political dead man. Get the fuck out of my office. All of you."

In the anteroom, Dan removed the cuffs from Hansen's wrists. "I think that you'd better find another job."

"You're not arresting me?"

"The record has been set straight. You may be called to testify, but you won't be charged with anything, unless you don't cooperate with the Pine County attorney."

"But the attorney general is going to take over the investigation," Hansen said.

"I doubt it," Sepanen replied.

. . .

When Williams and Sepanen arrived at the attorney general's office at three o'clock, the hallway was crowded. "Looks like your phone calls generated the desired response, Dan."

"Fat lot of good it does," Dan said. "We don't have a murderer."

"We've got a big rat in a tight cage, though," said Sepanen, with a self-satisfied grunt.

Capitol security was trying to keep the camera people and the news reporters back from the entrance to the attorney general's office. Sepanen walked in and introduced himself to the receptionist. A state trooper escorted them inside.

"Sheriff Sepanen!" The attorney general rose from his desk and offered his hand.

"This is Dan Williams," Sepanen said, "my undersheriff."

"Ah, yes, I've heard you've done some wonderful investigative work up north," the attorney general said, as he shook

Dan's hand.

"Thanks," Dan replied. "We're here to make you a hero today, Mr. Gray."

"Does that have something to do with the crowd outside?"

"We've called a press conference at three-ten to announce that we've cracked a kickback scheme involving Senator Petrich and Bell Gravel Company."

Gray's face went dead serious. "Oh, is that so? Well, maybe we'd better talk about that, don't you think? Maybe you'd better sit down." He motioned toward the overstuffed chairs just in front of his desk. Sepanen and Williams glanced skeptically at one another, then both sat down. So did the AG, resting his elbows on the huge polished surface of his desk.

"Uh huh. Now, gentlemen," said the AG, clearing his throat, "what's this all about? You know," he said, before they could answer, "I don't think what you intend to do is wise. You're aware, of course, that Senator Petrich is very influential and, besides, it could do a great deal of damage to a number of careers if you were to continue."

Williams glanced at Sepanen. Sepanen just smiled.

"Let's see now," continued the AG, apparently oblivious to their exchange of glances, "don't you think it would be better to just announce a joint investigation of your murder case, which will transfer to my investigators? It would solve so many of both our problems, don't you see? You can be sure that there will be consequences. You needn't worry about that."

Williams smiled. "I'm afraid it's too late for that, Mr. Gray. The *St. Paul Dispatch* and the *Minneapolis Star Tribune* are already in possession of signed depositions from a contract employee in the Pine County engineer's office. The head of capitol security and the Senate sergeant-at-arms just heard a confession from Senator Petrich's aide about the amount, logistics, and timing of the bribes."

Gray's face took on an alarmed expression.

"I suggest you join us in making this announcement," said Dan, "with a subsequent follow-up investigation by your office to determine the extent of the corruption."

Gray leaned slowly back in his high-backed executive chair. "I'm afraid that would be impossible," Gray said softly.

"Because of the unwritten DWI that Petrich has on your wife?" said Dan.

Gray just stared in shock at Williams and Sepanen. "I should have known," he said, finally.

"Why not announce that she's going into treatment?" said Dan. "It'll defuse the issue, Mr. Gray. The public can handle it."

Gray rose from his chair and walked to his office window, staring out at the crowd that had gathered there. "How widespread is the knowledge of my wife's DWI, Officer Williams?"

"I'm afraid it's folklore in the state patrol," Dan replied, "and I heard in the BCA, as well."

"Good God," Gray said, "We're ruined."

"Not if you meet it head-on," Sepanen again suggested. "Look at Betty Ford. Make it a character issue. Beat Petrich to the punch."

Gray turned and faced them. "Would you gentlemen mind waiting in the reception area for a few minutes while I make a couple of calls?"

Sepanen looked at his watch. "The news conference starts in

three minutes, with, or without you," he said. The two men rose from their chairs and walked to the door while Gray turned and stared out his window again.

Sepanen stopped at the door. "We'd rather be with you than against you on this, Tom."

When Gray turned from the window, tears glistened on his cheeks. "I appreciate that, John. I'm just going to call my wife and warn her. Then, I'll have to call the governor and tell him he's about to lose a senate committee chairman."

. . .

Williams, Sepanen and Gray walked together into the hallway and the blinding glare of the television lights. Gray stepped to the bank of microphones.

"Ladies and gentlemen, I want to introduce you to the sheriff and undersheriff of Pine County. This is Sheriff Sepanen, and this is Undersheriff Williams. Their office has just concluded a brilliant investigation that has exposed a corruption ring involving at least one state contract winner and the chairman of the Senate Transportation Committee." There was a murmur throughout the crowd. "Their investigation will show that ... "

Chapter 20

Dan Williams was up at 5:00 a.m., and on his way to Moose Lake ten minutes later. He ate a heavy breakfast at Dick's Cafe and bought another roll of Tums. He popped two into his mouth to counteract the coffee's attack on his stomach.

At 6:55 a.m. he pulled into Ann Olsen's driveway. The lights were on in the kitchen. Ann peered through the curtains, then opened the door. She wore a terry cloth robe that made her look round. The bandages were gone from her head.

"Deputy Williams," she said, with surprise. "What are you doing here?"

"I hope I didn't wake you up," said Williams.

"No, no. Not at all. Please come in. You didn't wake us up. Eric's on day shift this week and had to be in Askov for work at six. He woke the baby with the sound of his electric razor."

Williams sat down at the kitchen table while Ann brought the coffeepot and two mugs.

"How are you feeling?" Dan asked. "Are you still seeing two of me?"

Ann laughed. "I'm doing pretty well. My vision is still a little fuzzy. The doctor says it'll improve with time. The headaches are getting better, too." The smell of the hot, freshly brewed coffee filled the kitchen as Ann poured.

"I was just wondering if you might have remembered anything more about the attack." Dan said.

The smile that had lit her face turned quickly to a frown. She shook her head. "Not really. I was so scared that a lot of things just ran together. I can't even tell you the color of the ski mask the guy was wearing."

"Did he say anything to you?"

Ann took a big sip of coffee and thought hard. "I think so. But I hadn't really remembered that. It was something strange, like, 'so much for you', or something like that."

Williams paused to let her think for a while longer, but after a few seconds she shook her head. "I guess that's all I can come up with."

"I assume you know the intruder tried to kill you?"

Again, Ann frowned. "That's what Deputy Ryan said. She told me that's why you had her sit outside my hospital room."

"We're continuing to keep the house under surveillance. There's a deputy in the empty house next door every night." Dan waited for some protest, but none came. He added, "I have some bad news. They found Jean Oinen two days ago. She's dead."

Ann's face froze in disbelief and pain. "Oh, no. I can't believe it." Her eyes filled with tears. She pulled a handkerchief from the pocket of her robe and held it to her face as she sobbed. After a few moments she composed herself and asked, "What happened to her?"

"She was stabbed. The blood in the trailer was hers."

"Where'd they find her?"

"Two fishermen found her in Barnum. On the island in Bear Lake."

"But how'd she get there?" Ann asked.

Williams shook his head. "We don't know. We're trying to sort it all out." They sat in silence for a few minutes. "Have you thought any more about what she'd discovered? It may be the key to finding the killer," said Dan.

Ann shook her head. "I've thought about it a lot. But I still don't understand what she was saying."

"By the way; Jean didn't have an abortion when she disappeared that time," Dan said. "She had a baby girl ... in Willmar."

Ann looked very surprised. "I can't believe that. She told me she'd had an abortion."

"Apparently not," said Dan.

"What did she do with the child? Where is she?"

"We don't know that yet. We're working on it."

"So hard to believe," said Ann.

"How close were you and Jean?"

"Maybe not as close as I thought," said Ann, ruefully. "We talked a lot, and she invited me to some of her parties. As far as I was concerned, we were best friends."

"You were partners, too. Weren't you?"

Ann blushed and looked away. "No. What makes you say that?"

"We have witnesses, Ann, people who've said you were her partner," Dan said. "Jean wasn't a hostess for parties. She was a hooker. She was a victim. Were you a victim too?"

Ann suddenly got up from the table and walked to the window. She pulled back the yellow curtains and looked out into the muddy yard. When she turned back, her expression had grown even sadder.

"Do you have any idea how hard it is to live in this town and run into those men?" She stopped and turned to stare out the window again. "They act polite, but they look down on you, like you're a piece of trash. And maybe they're right. I try to play it all down. I try to act like it's nothing."

Ann came back to the table and took a drink of coffee. "You wanted to know how close Jean and I were. I don't suppose you've ever been naked in bed with two women? The women have to be pretty comfortable with each other to do a two-on-one. A few of the men really got off on that for a while. Some just wanted to see the two of us together. I thought it was a big laugh at first. We just playacted. Then, I could see it in their eyes; they thought it was real. I couldn't take it. The whole thing was dirty enough, but to think the men believed that Jean and I actually had that kind of relationship ... that was too much."

"Is that when you got out of it?" Dan asked.

Ann sighed and smiled wanly. Her eyes grew distant as her thoughts trailed back. "No," she said, after a moment, "I was in it too deep by then. Couldn't back away from the money. It was the only source of income I had. But I never got used to it, or accepted it. Then I met Eric and he fell in love with me. He took me away from it all."

"How'd Jean take that?"

She looked back at Williams. "Very well. She was happy for me. It was what we both dreamed of; that some knight in shining armor would come and take us away. Every guy who came through the door said he loved us, that he'd do anything for us." Her voice took on a note of bitterness. "Most of that is bullshit. But Eric was different, and that makes all of it even harder. Eric loves me, I'm sure, but the whole thing is a terrible strain on our marriage."

She got up from the table and brought the coffeepot back and refilled both their cups. "Any other part of my soul you want bared?" Ann asked.

"How does Eric feel about Jean, now that you're out of the business?"

"Jean and I didn't see each other after the wedding. Then she called one night and wanted to talk. Eric wasn't happy about it."

"Has he ever struck you?" Dan asked.

"No!" Ann said, emphatically. "What made you ask that?"

"Were *any* of the customers violent?"

Ann stopped and stared blankly until the implication of the question hit her. "Eric couldn't do that," she replied. "Eric is the most gentle man I've ever known. Most of the others were pretty gentle, too. There were a couple ... who liked to be rougher. They were mostly the young ones."

"Rougher? How?"

"You know. More aggressive."

"Violent?"

"Um." Ann stopped and tears welled in her eyes. "Just mean. You know, pinching, spanking, poking. Things like that."

"Jean put up with that?"

"Not really. She didn't let them come back."

"Some were rough with you?"

"Just once. Eric saw the bruises and beat the crap out of him."

"Who was *him*?" Dan asked.

Ann stared down at the front of her robe. "Jerry Walker."

Dan remembered Walker as one of the men he'd talked to earlier but made a mental note to check on him again. "Jean must have had some rough customers too, didn't she?"

"She did a couple of times. She showed me the bruises on her legs once. One time, she couldn't entertain for a couple of weeks until the bruises healed."

"What happened to the man?"

"I guess the word got out and caused a stir among the rest. They sorted it out. At least that's what I heard."

"Vigilante justice," Dan said. "Do you know who the man was?"

Ann shook her head, "No."

"How long have you been out of it?"

"About a year and a half."

"So, you were still in the business when Petrich started coming around?" Dan asked.

"Oh, yeah. But he was only interested in Jean. I used to be too skinny, if you can believe that." She smiled to herself. "Jean told me Petrich said he liked her because she had cleavage, especially after the breast implants."

"Was Petrich rough?"

"No, he was just on an ego trip. His whole thing was acting out a rape. He wanted to be in power. One night, Jean was too busy to see him, so I filled in. He couldn't even get it up until I pretended to be hard to get."

"Tell me about the doctor from Fond du Lac?"

"Oh, him! He was so scared he couldn't do it most times. We thought he might be gay and was only coming along for appearances. He only came a few times." Ann quickly looked at Williams to see if he had taken her comment as a pun. "Oh, I didn't mean ... "

Williams smiled weakly. "How about anyone else that was really scary?"

"Well, like I said, they policed themselves pretty well. Only people they trusted got into the group. If we got someone we didn't like, they got pushed out. We had one old guy that smelled really bad. Like he didn't ever take a bath. We told him to take a hike."

"Did Jean use condoms?"

"That was really weird," Ann said. "Jean never seemed worried about getting pregnant. I never allowed it without condoms. And I warned her."

"Anything else that you can tell me about Jean?"

"Jean was my sweetheart," said Ann, then, again, looked quickly at Dan to see if he had taken the comment wrongly. "You know what I mean. She was a sweetie to everyone. Poor Jean! I think that she actually really loved a lot of those guys. If any of them had ever asked her to run away, I think that she might have gone. I was in it for the money. I think, for Jean, it was more than that."

A baby's cry came from upstairs and Ann excused herself. She was back in a couple of minutes with the baby cradled in her arms. The boy had a cast on one leg. Ann cuddled the baby, smiling up at Dan. "Jean would have loved to have had a baby," she said, "That's why I can't believe she had a child and didn't tell me. I think that she felt her time was running out and her chances were passing by." Ann looked searchingly at Dan. "Maybe that's what she meant last time we talked," she said. "Maybe she had found someone who was going to marry her and take her away."

Dan took a sip of coffee, eyeing Ann over the rim of the cup. "Jean must have been a pretty poor judge of character," he said, "if she thought her killer was going to marry her and run away."

"Let's face it," Ann said, "a hooker … " she frowned at her own expression, "doesn't see a lot of people she would want to take home to mom. If Jean found someone, chances are he was kinda marginal anyway. Besides, when you want something very badly, your emotions get in the way. I was just lucky with Eric."

Williams looked at his watch and was surprised to see that it was nearly eight o'clock. "I've got to run," he said. "Thanks for the coffee and the information, Mrs. Olsen. You've been a big help." Dan stopped at the door. "We're going to open Jean's safe-deposit box, today. Would you have any idea what she has in it?"

Ann shrugged. "She was pretty sentimental, but she wouldn't keep anything personal in the trailer. I'm surprised she even had that picture of the two of us there. Maybe she has something like her old class ring, or love letters in there."

"Do you think it could be her old planners?" Dan asked.

"Jean liked to keep records of everything, but she kept them in her trailer as far as I know."

"Do you think it's possible that Jean might have been black-mailing someone?" asked Dan.

"You believe Jean was keeping records to blackmail some-one?" She laughed. "Jean was a dreamer, not a blackmailer. Jean wanted everyone to like her. She might blackmail them for that, but not money."

Dan took out his business card and held it out. "If you think of anything else, give me a call."

Ann didn't reach out to accept the card. "Sorry, but I'm not going to think about it for another minute. I spend all my time cleaning and taking care of the baby. I take baths two or three times a day. Do you know why?"

Dan shook his head.

"To get the filth off me," Ann said. "I'll never be dirty like that again."

Chapter 21

It was past nine o'clock when Dan arrived at the Pine Brook Bank. He scanned the lobby for William Peikert and finally saw him sitting with Rob Martin in the bank president's office. They saw Dan at the same moment and both men rose to meet him. Martin looked nervous.

"Have you got the court order and the key?" he asked. "If you don't have the key, we'll have to drill the lock. That'll take most of the morning to get the locksmith."

Williams reached into the inside pocket of his buckskin jacket and pulled out a piece of paper. He handed it to Martin. As Martin examined the court order, Williams pulled the key from the breast pocket of his plaid shirt. He examined the number 213 stamped into the brass.

Martin handed the court order to Peikert, the attorney, who waved it off. Martin held it nervously in his hand for a second. "I suppose that we should keep this in case anyone ever has any questions."

"You can," Dan said. "The court has a copy on file too." Martin set it on top of his desk and silently led them down the stairs into the basement of the bank.

In the basement was the open vault door exposing a grate blocking the door to the room with the safe-deposit boxes. Martin pulled a ring of keys from his pocket and unlocked the grate. They walked into the tiny room and scanned the wall of locked boxes until Martin found number 213. He inserted a key from his ring into one lock on the face of the box then put his hand out to Williams for the other key.

Both keys turned easily in the locks, and Martin pulled the door open exposing the gray face of the inner box, which had a metal ring on the front for a handle. He pulled the box out and handed it to Williams. "There are some tables in private cubicles around the corner."

The three of them marched to the first cubicle and set the box on the counter. "I hope there's something in here," Dan said. "It's awfully light."

Dan pulled up the lid, exposing a layer of fuzzy, pink fabric. He lifted the fabric and was surprised to find a doll, wearing a knit cap.

The banker leaned close. "That's weird," he said. "I've never seen anything in a deposit box like that. Is it just a doll?"

Dan lifted out the doll and pink blanket, laying them on the table. Under the doll were a number of papers. He lifted up the first, holding it so that the other two men could see the birth certificate. He read aloud, "Baby girl, Oinen. No given first name. Mother, Jean Marie Oinen. Father …" His hopes fell. "Unknown."

The next item was a picture, apparently taken in a hospital, of a newborn baby wrapped in a pink blanket. "This must be the baby," Dan said. "Looks like she's wearing the cap that's on the doll, and she's wrapped in a pink blanket."

Peikert shook out the tiny receiving blanket and compared it to the picture. "Miss Oinen was almost obsessed with finding her child. Every time she came to my office she seemed more and more intense. I tried to point out that the adoptive parents probably weren't interested in meeting her, or in having her see the girl. But she was determined."

Martin shook his head. "I asked the head teller about Jean. She was coming in more and more frequently to get into the box. The teller was really curious about what was going on, because she'd take the box out, then she'd sit in one of these cubicles, just talking to herself."

Williams leafed through the remaining papers. A few old birthday and Christmas cards signed, "Ann." The last item was a bill from the hospital in Willmar. Dan asked, "I wonder if this was ever paid?"

Peikert shrugged. "I'll check on it. If it's still delinquent, I'll pay it when I probate the estate."

"If it was paid," Dan said, "I'd like to know who paid it."

"Sure," Peikert said. "I'll ask that, too, and get back to you if I find anything."

Dan loaded the pieces back into the box and Martin returned it to its proper location. Williams handed the key to Peikert and said, "Since there doesn't appear to be anything pertinent to the murder in there, I'll leave this in your care."

. . .

Williams drove back to his office deep in thought. Why would an adult woman keep a doll in a safe-deposit box? Where are Jean's planners? Who fathered the baby Jean gave up for adoption? Did any of those questions have anything to do with her murder?

At his desk, Dan found a pink message slip asking him to call Laurie Lone Eagle. He dialed the number and waited. After five rings a female voice, not Laurie's, came on the line.

"Minnesota Bureau of Criminal Apprehension."

"I had a message to call Laurie."

"Is this Undersheriff Williams?" the woman asked.

"Yes."

"Hang on for a moment," she said. "Laurie asked me to interrupt her if you called."

While he waited, Dan pulled out the sociogram of Jean's clients. At the top he added a halo around Ann Olsen's name. He drew a line from Bell to Petrich, then studied the rest. "It all fits together too neatly," He said, to the hum on the phone.

"Dan?"

"Hi, Laurie. You called?"

"I thought that you'd want to know," she said. "Orrin Petrich was arraigned today on bribery charges."

"Great. Too bad it wasn't a grand jury considering murder charges."

"Hey, take the successes as they come. They're too few and far between. Are you making any progress on the Oinen murder?"

"No," Dan replied. "We opened the victim's safe-deposit box today, but all we found was a doll and a birth certificate."

"A doll? Why would she keep a doll in a safe-deposit box?"

"Jean Oinen had a baby when she was in high school and apparently gave it up for adoption. She was using a lawyer to help locate it before her murder. According to her lawyer, she was obsessed with getting the girl back. The certificate lists the father as unknown."

"You think the father might be the killer, then?"

"I don't know," Dan said. "Maybe he's just another loose end that I need to tie up. Maybe he'd lead me to something else. I just don't know."

"Could the doll be a collectible?"

"No, it was just a plain-old, plastic baby doll," Dan replied. "She had it dressed up in the clothes that were shown on the hospital picture of the baby she gave up for adoption."

"Sounds like she was a little messed up."

"Every hooker I've ever dealt with has been a little messed up," Dan said. "I talked to Jean Oinen's partner in this sex-ring this morning, and she's having her own problems, too. She tried to rationalize that she and Jean were only hosting parties. By the time we got through talking she was telling me about the multiple baths she has to take daily to cleanse herself from the 'filth,' as she put it."

"Yeah," Laurie said, "I've looked at some of the literature on that stuff. Seems like it's tough to get out of the business. It must be even more complicated in a small town."

"Going just by what I've learned from these two women, I'd say the literature is right on."

Laurie paused. "It sounds like the Oinen woman was really fixating on this baby, though."

"Yeah. I'm thinking it's a major angle in this case."

"Where do you go from here?" Laurie asked.

"Back to Fond du Lac. The ME says that whoever murdered Jean Oinen was skilled in anatomy, like a doctor. I've got to check him out, although the partner says she and Jean thought Rubenstein, the doctor, was gay."

"You're kidding me! What goes on behind closed doors, huh? Tell me some more about the partner."

"Ann Olsen? She was an old friend who used to turn tricks with Jean. Ann fell in love with one of the Johns and married him. She says Jean was envious of her happiness. Jean called her the night of the murder and told her she 'had it figured out,' to put it in her words. Ann can't understand exactly what that meant, but, apparently, Jean was going to call someone and tell him whatever it was that she'd figured out."

"Did you check the phone records to see if she'd made a long distance call?" Laurie asked.

"Shit!" Dan muttered. "I assumed it was local. Good idea. The BCA must be teaching you something, Laurie. You're getting too good."

Laurie chuckled. "You said the partner married one of the customers. How does the husband feel about Jean, the active prostitute, calling his wife, her former partner?"

"Ann told me he wasn't real happy about it. I don't see that as a strong motive, but he's still a possible suspect."

"Tell me about our gay doctor. Is he, really?"

"Jean's partner said Rubenstein showed up a few times, but

he always seemed uncomfortable. They suspected he was gay and that he just came along to keep up his image with the guys."

"Great gossip for the family get-together," Laurie laughed.

"All right, now. Be nice to the guy," Dan admonished. "He's the only doctor you've got up there on the res. Don't make him a pariah."

"I guess," Laurie said. "But that's just too juicy. I've heard a few things myself about the good doctor. His nurse told me he disappears three or four times a year, for a week at a time. He doesn't tell anyone where he's going, then just shows up again without an explanation. It drives her crazy trying to schedule around his travels."

"Hmmm. That's very interesting."

"Just gossip. Probably not important."

. . .

Dan dialed the phone company, gave the supervisor his iden-tification, and asked for a list of all the long distance calls made from the trailer, especially any on the evening of April 29th. He listened to the click of the keyboard as the clerk entered data. "I have the long distance billing on the screen for that telephone number. There is only one long-distance call shown in the last month, made on the twenty-sixth, to a number in Duluth."

"Can you tell me whose number was called?" Dan asked.

There was another series of clicks. "The Glass Block store in the Miller Hill Mall."

"Dead end."

"Excuse me?"

"Sorry," Dan said. "Just talking to myself."

Williams went to the records clerk. "I need to check for a file. Can you see if we have anything on Eric Olsen? That's Olsen with an E."

The clerk pulled up a file on the computer and typed in the name.

"Nothing," said the clerk.

"Try 'Walker, Jerry,' with a J or G."

The keys on the computer keyboard clicked. The clerk paused, then the screen filled.

"Bingo! We have Gerald, with a G. It looks like he's had a half-dozen arrests. I show two DWI convictions, one aggravated assault and a simple assault. Do you want me to pull the files?"

"No, thanks," Dan said. "Check on 'Rubenstein,' in Fond du Lac. I don't know the first name."

The clerk smiled. "I don't suspect there are many Rubensteins with Minnesota criminal records." She typed in the name and waited. "By golly! There are a half-dozen. Three in Minneapolis, two in St. Paul, and one in Thief River Falls. There aren't any criminal records for Rubensteins in Fond du Lac."

. . .

Williams drove to Fond du Lac and showed up at Dr. Rubenstein's office at one o'clock. He walked in and the receptionist/nurse recognized him immediately.

"I hear," she said with a smile, "that Mr. Senator Petrich got another shot in the rear today."

Williams gave her a quizzical look.

"The radio said Senator Petrich was arraigned on three counts of bribery," she said. "The Senate Ethics Committee is considering expulsion, too. Couldn't happen to a nicer guy. You have anything to do with that?"

"I helped out a little."

"I heard you were modest. Are you married? I've got a cute sister ... "

Williams put his hand up to stop her. "Happily married," he said. "Any chance that I can talk to the doctor before he starts seeing his afternoon patients?"

"For you, anything. You're my hero." She winked and led him down the hallway to where Rubenstein was sitting in a cramped office reading medical test reports at a cluttered desk.

"Dr. Rubenstein?"

The doctor looked up from the sheet he was reading and then, recognizing Williams, said with obvious irritation, "What do you want this time, Sheriff?"

Dan pulled the door shut and leaned against it, not seeing anywhere to sit. "I just need to ask you a few more questions. I understand you visited Jean Oinen and her *partner* at the trailer in Sturgeon Lake." He put the strong emphasis on the partner so Rubenstein would realize the extent of the investigation.

Rubenstein's face flushed red. "So what do you want to do? Throw me in jail for visiting a prostitute?"

"Where were you the evening of the twenty-ninth?"

"Well, Sheriff, I suppose that I was sitting in this office like I am most nights. When you're a staff of two, it gets a little busy.

I sit here most nights until nine or ten."

"Are you married?"

"Only to this job," Rubenstein replied. "What does my marital status have to do with anything?"

"I thought if you were married that perhaps a wife could offer an alibi."

"There's no wife, and there's no alibi, unless my nurse telling you how many files I had on my desk when she left at six would suffice."

"I'm afraid that won't do it," said Dan. "You've got to do better than that."

"Wait!" said the doctor, his face suddenly lighting up. "I *can* do better than that. I was still returning patient calls late. I could check to see who I called."

"There are phones all over the place," Dan said. "You could call from a cell phone and say you were in your office."

"Doesn't the phone company keep a record of all calls and where they originate?" Rubensein asked.

"Not on local calls," said Dan, "only long-distance."

The doctor stopped and nodded, somewhat crestfallen.

"When was the last time you saw Jean?" asked Dan.

"Several months ago. Ron Bell dragged me down there again."

"It wasn't voluntary?"

"Look, Williams, I'm not into that stuff," said the doctor, his irritation growing.

"Because you're gay?"

A look of shock appeared on Rubenstein's face. "Well, I'll be damned! No, I'm not gay. I'm just not into running around the countryside having sex with every prostitute I can find. Do you have any other impertinent questions?"

"You disappear for a week at a time, several times a year. Where do you go?"

Rubenstein sighed resignedly. "So that's it. This has nothing to do with Jean Oinen, does it? I thought I'd escaped the persecution when I left New York. I thought I was living among native people who could empathize. But no, they're as bigoted as the rest!" The doctor's shoulders slumped and he seemed even more weary than he had on Dan's previous visit.

"What in hell are you talking about?" Dan asked. "You already told me you're not gay, and I'm not into gay bashing, anyway. I'm conducting a murder investigation and the medical examiner suggested that the wounds on the victim were inflicted by someone with a very good knowledge of anatomy, like a doctor."

Rubenstein froze, as if attempting to understand what Williams had just said, then he started to laugh. He looked at Dan and asked, "So you seriously want to know where I go on my short vacations? I thought you were squeezing me because I'm a Jew."

"Jew shmew. I want to solve a murder."

"Well, Sheriff ," said the doctor, his spirits obviously rising, "those missing weeks? I go down to Minneapolis and stay with a Jewish family. I go at the same time every year: Rosh Hashana, Yom Kippur, Pesach and Hanukkah. Would you like the name of the family I stay with?"

"I don't think that will be necessary," said Dan, with some chagrin.

Rubenstein smiled. He was beginning to actually like this sheriff. "How was Jean murdered?" he asked.

"A small cut to the neck. The ME said the carotid artery was cut."

"The medical examiner thinks a doctor did it?"

"He said the person who had inflicted the wound had to have a good knowledge of anatomy, like a doctor."

"Well, that's a possibility,"Rubenstein said, "but there are others who would be able to do that kind of thing. You know, that's how they butcher kosher beef. The rabbi cuts the neck and lets them bleed out. Maybe you should be looking for a rabbi?" The doctor was obviously beginning to enjoy himself, now.

Williams hardly noticed, however. His imagination was fast rewinding over the fragmented facts of the case: an expertly cut throat; a butcher; a frozen body.

. . .

Williams stopped in Moose Lake on his way back to Pine City. Eric Olsen answered the door.

"Mr. Olsen? I'm Dan Williams, from The Pine County sheriff's department. I was wondering if I could speak with your wife. It's about the Jean Oinen murder investigation."

Eric Olsen looked Williams over, frowning, then turned back to the interior and called his wife's name. From the kitchen, Ann's voice came calling back. "Yes, what is it?"

"She'll be here in a little bit" said Olsen and wandered off, leaving Williams standing on the front step. Ann appeared at the door, wiping her hands on a dish towel, and quickly ushered him in. "Hello, Sheriff Williams. You'll just have to excuse Eric. I think sometimes that man has no manners at all."

Dan sat at the table. Ann pulled the coffeepot from the stove and poured two cups and sat down. "You've got more information about Jean?" she asked.

"We opened her safe-deposit box today."

"And?"

"And found a baby picture," Dan said, "and a doll, dressed just like the baby in the picture. There was a birth certificate for the baby and the father was listed as unknown. Does that mean anything to you?"

Ann Olsen took a sip of coffee before she answered. Dan noticed her hand shaking a little as she pressed the cup rim to her lips. "I told you I didn't want to think of these things anymore, Sheriff, but I can't keep from it. After you left, I began to remember some things I'd noticed about Jean, that didn't seem important at the time. But when you told me about the baby they began to make sense. Jean just seemed to be almost obsessed with holding our baby. She would hold him and take care of him every chance she got. She got almost possessive, and she was just constantly commenting on how happy Eric and I are. As I say, I noticed it, but made nothing of it at the time. But it fits with the doll you found. I didn't think it had gone that far, though."

"Apparently it did. You still don't have any idea about who she might have called that night?"

"You know," Ann replied, "I've wracked my brain, but I can't come up with a hint. You haven't got any other clues?"

"Not a one," Dan said. "Maybe someone will come forward

with something."

"Have you got any idea about who attacked me?"

Williams drew a deep breath. "We've got the samples of the drug that you were given being analyzed by the BCA. Beyond that, I'm assuming it had something to do with Jean."

"I can't see how. Don't you think it could have just been a botched burglary?"

"Maybe, but the drug angle is all wrong. There's something more. Can you think of anything that you haven't told us?"

Ann shook her head. "My life has been wonderfully dull since I married Eric."

"Where does Eric work?" Dan asked.

"The welding shop, in Askov. They make metal desks and file cabinets." Ann was looking at Dan suspiciously. "Why do you ask? Is Eric back to being a suspect again?"

"We just have to check out every angle, Ann," said Dan. "Has he ever worked in a butcher shop or drugstore?"

Ann looked at Dan blankly. "I don't think so."

Chapter 22

The dispatcher caught Dan as he pulled onto the freeway and asked him to meet the plumber at Jean Oinen's trailer. The Renquist Plumbing van was idling in front of the trailer when he arrived.

"Hi, Dan," Kip Renquist said. "I thought Sandy Maki was going to meet me."

"Sandy's on the night shift." Dan led Renquist past the crime-scene tape and unlocked the door. They were met with a blast of putrid air.

"Holy mama!" Renquist said. "That's worse than a backed-up toilet."

"If you think the smell's bad," Dan replied, "just wait 'till you get a look at it."

The bottom of the bathtub was caked with brown scum that had cracked when it dried. Dan pointed to the drain. "I need to pull any hair from the drain, then I want to collect whatever is in the drain trap."

"What are you looking for?" Renquist asked, holding his nose.

Dan shrugged. "I'll know when I see it."

After slipping on a pair of heavy rubber gloves, Renquist removed the mechanical stopper and with it, a long string of hair and goop. Dan held open a plastic evidence bag to collect the sample. Next, they pulled out the overflow drain plate. A long plug of hair, that resembled a drowned mouse, followed the mechanism out. Renquist placed it in a separate bag.

The plumber next slipped a narrow coiled spring down the drain and twisted it around as it plunged in and came back. It was covered with dark sludge, but no hairs or other masses.

"I guess that's all we'll get from here," Renquist said. "Let's do the trap. Do you know where the access panel to the crawl space is located?"

They walked around the outside of the trailer to a hinged panel. Dan noticed someone peering out through the curtains of the Youngquist's mobile home next door.

The plumber swung the panel aside and directed the beam of his flashlight under the trailer. He selected three wrenches, and climbed into the space on his hands and knees. Dan could hear the sound of scraping wrenches and creaking pipe joints.

"Hey, Dan, you want this stuff in evidence bags? You'll have to throw some under here."

"Anything interesting?" Dan asked as he pushed the bags under far enough for the plumber to reach.

"Just more goop," was the reply. "Here, grab the bags."

Dan got on his knees and reached under the trailer far enough to take the bags. As he braced himself against the inside of the skirting to balance, he felt what seemed to be a bulge under the insulation. Dan set the bags outside the skirting, then pointed his flashlight at the spot he had just touched. There were three bulges, and the insulation was secured over them with duct tape. He peeled the insulation back and found plastic bags sealed around a three-inch thick stack of papers. He held them to his chest as he backed out of the crawl space.

"Kip, I'll be in my squad."

"Okay, Dan. I'll close this up and be out in a second."

Williams carried the packages to the squad and examined them closely. Through the plastic he could see that each three-inch stack represented one year. The pages were punched to fit in some type of ringed binder. He selected the stack for the year 1998 and opened it.

As he leafed through the pages, he read the neat handwriting and meticulous record keeping of Jean Oinen. On the left side of each page was one week, broken down by the day and hour. Names were written as if for appointments, and in some spots there was a single word: *bank ... lawyer ... groceries*. On other lines, there was a name, *Ann*. It was Jean's way of keeping her appointments separate from Ann's.

On the right-hand side, on simple, ruled paper, were notes: "Ed, sick/cancelled" ... "Buy Scotch for Merle" ... "No ice for Orrin" ... .

Page after page was much the same as he looked through the stack. In the record for November, he found a note: "Orrin early, sent away. Came back mad, hit me. #2, last chance."

In the back of the stack was an alphabetical index with names. No phone numbers were listed. Apparently she didn't need to call; they called her. After each name was a note indicating preferences for what types of food and drink each man liked or disliked. Under Ron Bell's name was the note, "Allergic to strawberries—gets hives."

Kip Renquist loaded his tools back in the van while Dan quickly scanned the pages. He set the book aside as Kip stripped off the rubber gloves.

"I buttoned up the skirting," the plumber said. "Do you need me for anything else?"

"That should do it, Kip. Send the bill to the sheriff."

Renquist looked at the stack of papers Dan was still holding. "Is that what you pulled out of the insulation? It looks like an appointment book."

Dan smiled. "It's pure gold."

As Renquist pulled away, Dan turned to the entry with the name of Orrin Petrich. In Jean's neat handwriting it read: "From: Ron Bell. Likes Scotch. Likes food!" In different ink was the note, "mean." In pencil after that, was a note: "One strike." Then, in pen: "Two strikes."

He quickly leafed through the other names. At first it appeared that no one else even had one strike. Then, he noticed the names of Carl Johnson and Carl Johnson Jr. Next to "Junior" were the notes:"One strike," "Two strikes," "Three strikes."

He closed up the pages and looked through the other stacks, but the stack for the current year wasn't there. It made sense. The stacks he held in his hands were not current. The current stack was still in use and the killer had probably taken it.

He turned back to 1997 packet and found the names of Carl Johnson Junior and Carl Johnson Senior again. Carl Senior was listed as "From Al Westerman." Carl Junior was listed as "From

CJ Sr." Williams searched through his memory, trying to come up with a face to connect to the names, but couldn't.

He started the car, then turned it off, and walked back to the front steps of the trailer. The knob didn't turn, but the key was in his pocket. He unlocked the door and the blast of warm putrid air hit him like a wet blanket. He fought off the urge to walk away, and closed the door behind him. Nothing had changed except for the intensity of the smell.

In the bedroom he looked at the head of the bed. On the crossbar he found the slight dent in the dark wood where Oresek had found the hairs stuck in dried blood. He sat down at the desk and rifled through the scraps of paper again. Nothing.

"Jean, talk to me. Who was it?" he said, softly.

He stared at the phone for a second and then picked it up to look at the slip of paper under the receiver where most people write frequently called numbers. It was blank. He was about to set it down when he saw the "redial" button. He lifted the receiver and pushed "redial." The tones sang out the last number that Jean Oinen had called before she died.

Dan's pulse increased as the phone rang. Once. Twice. Three times. A woman's voice came on the line.

"Willow River Veterinary Clinic."

Williams froze.

"Hello. Is someone there?"

"Hi, Grace. This is Dan Williams. Is Ted around?"

"No, Sheriff Williams. Dr. Gapinski's on a call, but I expect him back soon. He still has a couple of people waiting for their four o'clock and four-fifteen appointments. We're running late."

Williams looked at his watch. It was nearly 5:30 p.m.

"Thanks, Grace."

"Should I tell him you called?" she asked.

"No," Dan replied. "I'm going to stop by in a few minutes. I'll surprise him."

He set the phone down in a daze. Oresek had said to find someone familiar with anatomy. Someone that might have surgical gloves at hand. He walked quickly to the squad and turned Jean's planner to Gapinski. "Ted Gapinski. Likes Miller Lite." There was no note of "From" under his name.

"Was he the first, Jean?" Dan asked.

He opened the other planners. All the other names were noted as being from someone else. In the earliest book, he went to Gapinski and it had the same notation. He quickly went back through the pages looking for Ted's name. On June 18, he found a note next to "Ted" after a nine o'clock visit. "Paid for Willmar."

Williams picked up the radio mike and called the dispatcher.

"Is the sheriff still in his office?" he asked.

"I think so. Hang on."

John Sepanen's voice came on the radio. "What do you need, Dan?"

"Can you find a judge to write a search warrant tonight?"

"They've probably gone home," the sheriff replied. "Can it wait until tomorrow?"

"Drag one away from his supper if you have to."

"Where do you need to search and what for?"

"Call me at … " he dug for the slip of paper with Jean Oinen's phone number. "I'll give you the details."

Chapter 23

Williams was sitting in the Willow River Veterinary Clinic waiting room with a woman comforting a dog of mixed lineage. The dog had a snout full of porcupine quills.

It was nearly six o'clock. The woman said she had been waiting since her four-fifteen appointment. The other people who had appointments after four-fifteen had left, she said, after rescheduling for another day. Apparently the dog had reconciled himself to the quills in his nose. He lay relatively quiet at the woman's feet. The woman petted the dog's head constantly and made soothing sounds when he moved. He would look up at her with big, sad eyes.

Ted Gapinski flew into the waiting area looking like he'd been rolled in manure, an odor emanating from him which attested to that very fact.

"Sorry I'm late. Damned cattle don't schedule their calf deliveries very well." He was focused on the woman with the dog and didn't notice Williams, sitting somewhat off to the side of the room, as he passed through.

Grace, the veterinary assistant, came in from the back and

asked the woman to bring "Bingo" into the back. Williams sat quietly, drinking strong coffee, eating Tums, and reading a *Minnesota Sportsman* forecast of the upcoming walleye-fishing season opener.

Gapinski appeared behind the counter in a clean set of tan coveralls. "Dan! What are you doing here?"

"I'm hooked on the coffee." Dan held up his ceramic mug filled with the vile liquid.

"I don't have any time to talk right now. Bingo's got a mug full of quills."

"Pull away," Dan said. "I'm not in any rush."

"Well, what do you need?" Gapinski asked. "I'm going to be awhile."

"I just wanted to talk about a fishing trip to Bear Lake."

"Go home and have some supper. I'll give you a call later."

"Sally's out with her friends. I'll hang around, if it's all right with you."

"Suit yourself. Shouldn't take too long." Gapinski disappeared into the back.

At six-twenty, Bingo came out, followed by his owner. Gapinski was a step behind.

"Do what you can to keep him quiet for the next few days," Gapinski was saying. "It'll take that long before his nose starts to feel okay again. And be sure to give him the pills so he doesn't get infected."

Dan looked at the snout of the big dog. It was obviously swollen. Bingo nervously focused on his owner's face, apparently anticipating a quick escape from this torture chamber.

"We'll see how smart Bingo is the next time he runs into a

porcupine," Gapinski said. "If he turns tail and runs, we'll know that he learned a lesson. If he doesn't, he may have a case of terminal dumbness."

The woman gave him a disbelieving look. "You mean some dogs do this more than once?"

Gapinski smiled. "I had a big old St. Bernard from Barnum that was in here once a year with a mouth full of quills. Every time the owner brought her in he swore that he'd shoot her before he'd bring her back again for the same problem. I guess his wife always twisted his arm to have her patched up one more time."

Bingo left, and Gapinski collapsed into a chair in the waiting area. "What a day. I've still got a horse that I should go check on." He let out a sigh. "But I can't get up again."

"I know the feeling," said Dan. "There are some things that just take it out of you, aren't there?"

Grace headed out the door, bundled in her coat. "See you tomorrow, Ted. Bye, Dan." They gave her a wave.

"You wanted to talk fishing? Why Bear Lake? Walleyes open on Saturday. I thought that you always went to Mille Lacs or Pokegama for the opener?"

"I used to," Dan said, "but they're so busy at the boat launches on the opener. I thought that maybe I'd hit Bear Lake for crappies."

"Well, there is that. And once in a while you can get a northern pike or two. But still, Sand Lake or Sturgeon are a little more productive."

"I heard that Bear was doing pretty good. Weren't you out there last week?"

Gapinski froze only for an instant, but enough for Dan to notice, then he rolled back into his friendly chatter. "Not lately. I don't think that I've been out on Bear in twenty years. I used to go out with an uncle and cousin. But that was before they filled in the northwest corner when they put the freeway through. Killed the fishing for a couple of years. The Department of Natural Resources would never let anything like that go through these days."

A thought jumped in Williams' head as he fought a delaying action. "Say, Ted. Do you know Carl Johnson?"

Gapinski made a face. "You want to go fishing with Carl Johnson?"

"You *do* know Carl Johnson," Dan said.

"I think I know four or five Carl Johnsons. The one from Kettle River does a little fishing, but most of the others aren't into fishing. At least not so that they talk to me about it."

Williams fought to hide his frustration. "The Carl Johnson who used to visit Jean Oinen."

"Oh, him. I don't think he does much fishing. At least he's never said anything about it."

"His son, Carl Junior, had some trouble with Jean. What happened?"

Gapinski paused, looking at Williams uneasily. "I don't remember anything about that. At least Jean never said anything to me about it."

In the distance was the sound of sirens. The wails were slightly out of sync, like two hounds baying.

Gapinski said, "Don't you need to check in, or something? I hear sirens."

Williams shrugged. "If they need me, they'll find me." Dan pressed on with his question. "Didn't something happen to Carl Junior? I can't quite remember, was it a car accident? What was it?"

"I can't remember Carl Junior at all, Dan." Gapinski said, Glancing at Dan curiously. "So, you think we should fish Bear Lake for the opener?"

"It's a thought. You got a better suggestion?"

Gapinski looked at the window. The sirens were very close. "Not really. Well, maybe I'd like Sturgeon Lake better. There's a little more boat traffic, but better fishing. Maybe Oak Lake would be good, too. It's got a few walleyes, and not too much fishing pressure."

"Yeah, and we can catch bullheads, if we get bored."

Gapinski heard the sirens stop just outside. "The Sturgeon launch is okay. Why do you ask?"

"Is that the launch just down from the mobile home park?" Dan asked.

Gapinski stood up and looked out the window. He saw an unmarked and a marked county squad roll to a stop in the driveway. "Uh, yeah. It's about a quarter-mile from there. Say, that's Sepanen coming up the sidewalk. Is he looking for you?"

Williams sat up and twisted to look. "I guess he found a judge that would issue a search warrant during his supper."

"Search warrant for what?" the vet asked.

Williams rose and walked to the door. Gapinski followed. They met the sheriff and Floyd Swenson. Williams held the door open for the two, and then allowed Sepanen to serve the warrant.

"We're here to search for evidence in the Jean Oinen murder, Ted." The sheriff said as he handed the search warrant to the vet.

"What?" Gapinski asked. "Why here?"

"Because you killed her," Dan replied, "and I'm thinking there is still some evidence lying around that might convict you."

Gapinski's face went white and he struggled to maintain his poise. Tiny drops of perspiration were starting to form on his bald pate. "*Killed* her? My God, Dan, you can't be serious. That's ludicrous! I haven't seen her in months!"

"Then why is your phone number the last one she dialed before she died?" Dan asked.

"You couldn't ... she didn't ... " Gapinski stood silent with his mouth open waiting for the right words to form. They didn't come.

"Floyd," Dan said over his shoulder to Sergeant Swenson, "I'll bet there's a big freezer in the back."

Williams looked at Gapinski, who nodded agreement. "I use it to store carcasses until the rendering service picks them up. Sometimes I have to save organs and animals for testing at the University. What's the big deal?"

"Get a picture of the inside, then check it for blood and human hairs."

Gapinski was regaining his wits. "Now wait a second. There's blood all over the inside of it. There's some from cattle, dogs, cats, and probably a horse." Gapinski paused, then added, "Hell, there might even be some of mine in there. Sometimes I nick myself."

"What we're interested in is human, B-positive, with anti-Kell," Dan said, "and any strands of brown hair."

Floyd Swenson walked behind the counter and into the back room.

"Now, Ted," Dan explained, "you and I and John are going to check your boat. I'll bet that there are a few strands of hair, and maybe some blood in it. The way I figure it, Jean Oinen has been in there twice, and if she has, there has to be something left behind."

Gapinski took a deep breath and appeared to be on the verge of protesting again. Then he turned and led Dan and the sheriff to the three-stall garage. Williams pulled open the first garage door and exposed a Chevrolet pickup with a topper. The sides were painted with the logo for the clinic. In the next stall was a Chevrolet Lumina, and in the last stall, a Lund fishing boat on a trailer.

Sepanen worked his way around the front of the Lumina, then walked around the perimeter of the boat, closely inspecting the gunwales for any hair or blood. At one point, he stopped and took a picture before plucking something from the edge. He dropped it into a tiny plastic envelope. Gapinski watched with growing consternation as the sheriff marked the bag with the time, location and description.

"It appears to be human hair and blood," the sheriff said, as he dropped the evidence bag into his pocket.

Williams was looking through junk piled around the back of the garage. He spied a canvas tarp and took a picture. He tried to unfold it in the cramped space. "Hey John,. I've got a tarp that smells like blood." He took a picture of it, opened.

"Of course it has blood on it," Gapinski said, gruffly. "I use it for doing barnyard surgery. Sheriff, what the hell is going on here?"

Both officers ignored Gapinski as Williams scraped samples from the tarp into plastic evidence bags, labeling each carefully. The sheriff, now inside the boat, was taking pictures of the live well and the stowage compartments. He stopped at a brown stain on the blue carpeting.

"I've got what appears to be a bloodstain on the carpeting here, too," the sheriff said. The flash from the camera lit the garage.

Gapinski was beside himself. "Of course there's bloodstain in my fishing boat! You think catching fish is bloodless? Maybe you should belong to PETA."

The sheriff's head disappeared as he bent down to scrape samples from the carpeting into an evidence bag. Williams had worked his way to the corner of the garage, followed closely by Gapinski. A cast-iron stove stood in the corner behind the boat. Gapinski watched in horror as Dan opened the door and looked into the stove. "I see some red leather ... "

The crash startled Sepanen, who had been on his hands and knees trying to scrape up some of the blood from the carpeting in the boat. "What the hell?" Running footsteps caught his attention, and he looked up in time to see Gapinski round the car and open the driver's door of the pickup. Dan was not in sight.

"Hold it!" The sheriff shouted.

Gapinski was in the truck and the engine roared to life before Sepanen could get out of the boat. He pulled his Smith &

Wesson .38 Special, but couldn't get a clear shot before the truck screeched out of the garage. Sepanen rushed to the door and watched the truck fishtail onto the road, turning north. He rushed back into the garage and found a dazed Dan Williams sitting next to the stove, rubbing his head.

"What happened to you, Dan?"

"I was looking into the stove when I got pushed. Banged my head pretty good. Where's Ted?"

"Headed north in the pickup," the sheriff said as he helped Dan to his feet.

Chapter 24

The sheriff picked up the radio mike. "Dispatch, we have a murder suspect northbound on County 61. He's driving a late-model, blue Chevrolet pickup, with matching topper. The doors of the pickup have the Willow River Veterinary Clinic logo."

"Ten-four," the dispatcher acknowledged. "I'll notify the state patrol and Carlton County."

"Better get an electronic TWIX out too. There's a lot of miles of empty roads he could travel."

"Ten-four."

Williams was in his squad, and in pursuit as the sheriff called in the bulletin. Dan saw Floyd Swenson running out of the clinic as he switched on the lights and siren. As Dan exited the driveway, he switched the radio to the state-wide frequency, used for pursuits.

"Pine County 608"

"Go, 608," the dispatcher responded on the new frequency.

"The suspect is armed. He has a .357 magnum that he uses to put down cattle."

"All units please note that Pine County is in pursuit of a murder suspect, last seen northbound on County 61. The suspect is armed."

Williams accelerated hard, knowing that the vet had a two or three minute head start. The squad would give Dan an advantage of twenty-five miles an hour on a straightaway, but there were a lot of side roads that could provide an escape route.

"Pine County 611"

"Go, 611" The dispatcher acknowledged Floyd Swenson.

"Floyd, I'm taking the turn to the freeway. Stay on sixty-one, toward Moose Lake."

"Got it, Dan."

Williams wheeled the squad around the corner in downtown Sturgeon Lake and sped toward the freeway. Dan asked himself which way to turn at the freeway, north, south, or straight-ahead? Toward the lake and eventually Wisconsin?

A Moose Lake officer announced, "I'm at Sand Lake Road and your suspect has not come this far north. I'll stay here."

"Ten-Four." Floyd Swenson passed downtown Sturgeon Lake and would meet the Moose Lake squad within minutes if they didn't intercept the vet before they met.

The dispatcher announced, "The state patrol has a plane up over Carlton. They are moving it southbound with a squad. He's in Air One. Carlton County is also southbound on the freeway from Barnum. Sandy Maki is northbound on the freeway from Pine City."

Williams rolled his squad to a stop at the top of the freeway overpass and sat waiting for the next report. Gapinski would be seen shortly if he was going either direction on the freeway.

Floyd announced, "I have Moose Lake PD in sight. I'm turning around. I'll go west out of Sturgeon Lake."

The sheriff was on the radio next. "I'm eastbound on Dago Lake Road. I'll check the side roads into the state forest for fresh tracks."

The radio grew silent as the net tightened; but was the fish in the net?

A small, Cessna airplane came into view over the north horizon. Dan swung the car crosswise on the bridge and flashed his headlights at the plane. The wings of the Cessna waggled. As it passed overhead, Williams saw the state patrol insignia on the side.

Williams turned off the red lights and started east across the freeway, toward the lake and mobile home park.

State patrol Air One announced, "I just met a Pine County squad south of Willow River. The freeway is clear."

"Air One," Dan radioed, "this is Pine County. Make a circle around Sturgeon Lake."

"Ten-four."

Dan stopped at the lake and looked across the gray, choppy water. A cold spring wind rippled through the still-bare limbs of the trees. A few ducks made a low pass before deciding to make a landing near the shore.

Dan pulled the squad to the right and drove past the mobile home park entrance. There was no blue truck in sight. It had been a long shot.

Air One announced, "Pine County, I have a blue pickup with blue topper eastbound on the south shore of Sturgeon Lake."

"Ten-four, Air One. We're on it." As Williams accelerated out of the mobile home park he spotted the plane across the lake.

"Air One, I've got you in sight. Stay with the truck."

The dispatcher announced, "Sepanen is east of Dago lake, and Maki is eastbound out of Willow River, parallel to Williams."

"Swenson, are you to the freeway yet?" Dan asked.

"I just crossed the freeway. I'm behind a state patrol by about two-hundred yards."

Air One announced, "The truck is now southbound."

As Williams turned south, the radio came alive again. "This is Air One. The suspect vehicle is now eastbound. It must be on County 46, headed toward Kerrick."

Williams cranked the wheel hard as he rounded the corner onto 46. The last transmission from the plane was less than a minute earlier. He had to be within a mile of the truck. As he came over a rise he could see the plane.

Dan rounded a corner as they approached the town of Kerrick and saw the pickup ahead. "This is Williams, I have the suspect vehicle in sight. We're at Kerrick."

The sheriff announced, "Maki and I are just south of Kerrick. We should be right behind 608 in a minute."

Dan sped up close behind the pickup and then eased into the left lane so Gapinski could see the red lights in the grille of the brown, unmarked squad. Gapinski's terror-stricken face was visible in the big side mirror.

Williams dropped back a bit and looked at his speedometer. They were travelling eighty-nine miles an hour. It was probably the top speed for the big, four-wheel drive pickup. It wasn't even taxing the engine in Dan's Crown Victoria. In the rear-view mirror, Dan caught sight of the other two squads.

Gapinski's plan suddenly hit Williams. "Dispatch, he's going to make a run for the state forest. We haven't got a chance on the muddy roads against his four-by-four. I'm going to bump him."

Williams accelerated hard until he was inches behind the truck where the driver's visibility was limited. He snapped the steering wheel left and shot past the rear of the truck. When his front wheels were past the truck's, he cramped the wheel hard to the right, pushing both vehicles toward the ditch as their tires screeched.

Gapinski fought the push but couldn't get the truck back to the left. The truck hit the ditch, locked together with the Crown Victoria, creating a spray of muddy water.

Dan's first sensation was that his feet were cold. He looked down and saw the muddy water rushing in around them. He tried to open the door, but the pressure of the mud and water provided too much resistance. He sat for a second, collecting his wits, then remembered to roll the window down. He climbed out of the window and stepped into the thigh-deep,cold water.

Sepanen and Sandy Maki were at the driver's door of the pick-up, pulling on the door handle—but the driver's door was jammed. Sepanen suddenly threw a shoulder into Maki as he yelled, "Gun!"

BOOM! The glass from the pickup window exploded into a million crystals as Sepanen and Maki fell sprawling into the ditch.

Clack. Thud. Clack. The distinctive sound of a pump shotgun ejecting a spent cartridge and chambering another caught each officer's attention.

Still standing in the water, Williams shook off the grogginess. He ducked behind his squad and struggled through the mud to the passenger door of the pickup. He crouched slightly behind the cab.

Sepanen and Maki slid through the muddy ditch and crouched in front of the truck. You okay, Sandy?" The sheriff asked.

The young deputy was shaking visibly. "I can't tell," Maki replied. "Nothin' hurts. I must be alive."

Williams leaned his back against the side of the truck and held his Smith & Wesson .45 automatic next to his shoulder. "Give it up, Ted, before someone gets hurt."

"Aaauugggh!" The scream came from inside the pickup.

Williams peeked around through the passenger's window for a split second, then holstered the gun and pulled the passenger door open. In what appeared to be slow motion he watched Gapinski push a hypodermic needle into his own abdomen. Williams reached to take it away, but too late. The plunger had already pushed the liquid out of the syringe.

"What was in the syringe, Ted?" Dan asked as he pulled the syringe from Gapinski's hand.

"It doesn't matter, Dan. I didn't have time to try for a vein. But, it's going to work anyway. Just more slowly."

Dan leaned out the door of the truck. "Sandy, call Airlink One. I've got the gun," he said, as he pushed the shotgun out the door into the mud.

"Why, Ted?" Dan asked. He picked up a clear glass vial with the rubber stopper from the seat. It had a warning label: "Beuthanasia-D Special (phenobarbital), for veterinary use only."

Gapinski leaned back, his face relaxing into a peaceful expression. "I'm not going to rot in prison, Dan," the vet said. "I couldn't handle it. I'd rather let the drugs ease me away. Saves the taxpayers a lot of money, you know."

Sepanen leaned in through the missing window. "Airlink One is in the air, and Moose Lake has an ambulance coming, too. Both are ten minutes out, or more."

Gapinski turned to look at the sheriff's face. "Too late, John. I can feel the relaxation coming now. I didn't hurt you, did I? I was aiming high. Just wanted to slow you down a bit."

"We're okay. What's up?" Sepanen asked Dan.

Williams handed the sheriff the vial. "In the belly."

Gapinski's eyes were closed. "Ted. You still here?" Dan asked.

Ted's eyes came open slowly. "Oh, yeah." The voice was groggy, like a drunk. "I always wondered if the animals felt much when we put them down. It's really not too bad. Except for the stick in the belly. That hurt like hell."

Dan asked, "Why'd you kill her, Ted?"

The vet's head lolled. "She was trying to push me into marrying her. She thought she was going to find our baby and get it back from the adoptive parents." He shook his head like he was trying to shake off the grogginess. "I tried to tell her that adoptions were final, but she was crazy. She told me she was going to kidnap the kid and she wanted me to help her. When I said 'no' she went nuts."

The vet's words came slower and slower. "I couldn't do any of that. After Emily died, I couldn't bear having another nagging wife." Gapinski's eyes closed and the breathing grew shallow.

Williams shook him. "Wake up, Ted!"

Gapinski's eyes popped open.

"Let's set the record straight, Ted. You killed Jean. Right?" Dan asked, hoping the vet was alert enough to answer.

"Yes," Ted replied, "Jean, too."

"Jean, *too*? There are others? Who else?" Williams shook Gapinski's shoulders and his head rolled to one side. "Who else, Ted? *Who else*?"

"Emily," he said, softly. "Maybe Ann ... I don't know."

"Emily?" Dan asked. "Emily died of a reaction to the penicillin."

The breathing was shallow, and Gapinski's eyes didn't open. The vet's lips opened and a whisper came out. "She was going to divorce me, Dan. The clinic was joint property. She was going to take me for everything. I had to save the clinic. Couldn't let her ruin me. It was just a little shot. No one ever knew, not even Emily. She trusted me and just let me give her that little shot."

"Shot of what?"

"Doesn't matter. Her body rejected it." His concentration was fading. Williams felt for a pulse. It was weak and under five beats in fifteen seconds.

"Ted, what can I give you to stop this? Is there something in the case? You don't want to die do you?"

"Too late, Dan. You're too late. Can't get a stimulant fast enough." Gapinski shook his head like a drunk in an argument. His eyes were closed.

"What Ann are you talking about Ted?"

"Pretty, blonde Ann," Ted replied. "Got a little fat didn't she?"

"Do you mean Ann Olsen? Jean's partner? She's not dead."

"Should've been. Almost killed me with that damned shotgun. Beat her head and stuffed her with pills. Should've been dead. Should've ..."

Gapinski's eyes closed and a slow breath expelled. A new breath was drawn slowly then a rattle came from the vet's throat as it shut down.

Williams put his fingers on the vet's neck, but he knew there wouldn't be a pulse. He pulled open an eyelid, and the pupil was fully dilated. Ted Gapinski was dead.

Chapter 25

S ally Williams rolled over and punched the button on the alarm clock. At some point during the night, she'd heard Dan come home, but she hadn't put on her glasses to see what time it was. She climbed out of bed and went into the shower. Dan never stirred.

She watched "Good Morning America" while she ate breakfast. The topic of the day was juvenile crime in America. They interviewed several street gang members from L.A. There was, of course, no mention of Pine County where juvenile crime was almost nil.

"What do we know that they don't?" she asked the television screen.

She returned to the bedroom and started dressing for work, when Dan rolled over and opened an eye. The left side of his face had been against the pillow. When he rolled over she saw the bruise.

"Oh, honey! What happened to you?" She sat down on the edge of the bed and touched the blue-black bruise on his cheek.

"Whacked my head on the car window when I ran off the

road," Dan replied. "They took x-rays. It's nothing."

"Looks nasty. I hope you make it clear that I had nothing to do with this." She smiled weakly, trying to make light of something that could be quite serious.

"Everyone knows already." He sat up in the bed and leaned back against the headboard. "Ted Gapinski's dead."

Sally leaned back and stared at him in shock. "What happened?" She asked, "A break in?"

"Suicide." Dan said.

"But why? Despair over Emily's death?"

"No," Dan said softly. "He killed Emily and Jean Oinen. He tried to kill Ann Olsen, too."

Sally stared in disbelief, unable to even come up with a question.

Dan explained, "Jean was trying to find a daughter she'd given up for adoption years ago. Ted was the father. She was pressuring him into marrying her and getting the child back."

"And he killed her for that?"

"Hey!" Dan said defensively. "I don't get it either. Maybe she went crazy and started to attack him and he lost it. Most murderers aren't rational anyway."

"Tell me about Emily."

"That's a new one on me. He said she was going to divorce him and take the clinic. He said it would have ruined him."

Sally gave him a look of disbelief.

"Hey, that's what Ted told me with his dying breath. I'm going to head over to his office this morning and try to get some more answers."

He pulled back the sheets, exposing the bruises on his legs

and torso from the crash. As he swung his legs from the bed he let out a grunt of pain. "Boy, it sure didn't hurt that bad last night."

Sally surveyed his bruised body. "Maybe you should stay put and let yourself heal a little," she said.

He stood up and walked stiffly toward the bathroom. "Naw. This is too crazy. I've got to find some answers."

. . .

Dan's squad pulled into the veterinarian's parking lot at 8:30 a.m. The only other car in the small parking area behind the combination house and veterinary office belonged to Ted Gapinski's assistant, Grace.

In the office, Grace was typing an invoice on the computer. "Hi, Dan. Ted's not around. Would you care for a cup of coffee?"

She got up and immediately poured a cup of the thick, black liquid without waiting for a response. "Ted must've had an emergency call early this morning," she said. "His truck was gone already when I got here at seven-thirty."

Williams gingerly sat down in a chair as Grace watched. "Are you okay, Dan?"

"I guess." He shifted uncomfortably in the chair, trying to find a position that didn't hurt. "I got banged up a little yesterday." Once he settled, Dan said, "Ted won't be in, Grace."

Grace's face was concerned as she handed Dan the cup of coffee. Dan accepted the cup and motioned for Grace to sit in the chair next to him. "Ted died yesterday afternoon."

Grace searched Dan's face for any hint of humor, and then realized he was completely serious. "Dead? How?"

"Ted gave himself an injection of Beuthanasia." Dan searched through his jacket pocket and handed the empty vial from the truck to Grace. She took it in her hand and spun it around so the label was visible.

When she looked up she had tears in her eyes. "But why, Dan?" she asked.

"Grace, Ted killed Jean Oinen and didn't want to spend the rest of his life in Stillwater prison."

"Oh, God," Grace gasped. She got up, walked to the counter, and pulled a box of tissues from a drawer. After drawing out a wad of the tissues, she buried her face in it and blew her nose. After a few seconds she returned to the chair and stared at Williams.

"I can't believe Ted killed Jean. He was a little temperamental, but he wasn't ... a *murderer*." The full implications of Dan's revelations were beginning to sink in; she had been working for a killer.

"He admitted it to me as the injection was taking hold."

Grace tried to say something, but the words didn't come.

"I have to ask you a few questions, Grace," said Dan.

After a few seconds, she nodded. "Sure. I guess ... I'm okay now."

"Do you keep track of the drugs? Or, did Ted do that himself?" Dan asked.

"I filled all the inventory and kept the books," she replied. "Ted doesn't like to do things like that. He said his job was being the doctor, and all the clerical stuff was mine."

"Have you noticed any discrepancies in your stock of drugs over the last couple of years?"

"What's a discrepancy?" Grace asked. "Ted took stuff out all the time and used it. I just reordered stock when it was down. There was no reconciliation of what we used against what was in stock."

"But, you kept the billings, too. Isn't there some way of checking what he was charging for against what was used?"

"We get a lot of stuff in-bulk," Grace said, "like tetracycline and chloramphenicol. There's no tracking that at all. He'd use one hundred grams on a horse then a few milligrams on a cat. I'd just order when we got low. Some of the other stuff we'd watch more closely, like the narcotics and the more expensive antibiotics."

"Did Ted take any barbiturates out of stock a couple weeks ago?" Dan asked. The coffee was starting to cause heartburn and he took two Tums.

"No. I don't think so." Grace searched her memory. "Oh, wait. I do remember Ted saying he had diarrhea … and he did take some Lomotil to stop it."

"What's Lomotil?"

"It's a drug we give to slow down the trots."

"How does it work?" Dan asked.

Grace shrugged. "Just a second." She disappeared into the back and returned with a box and a dangling sheet of paper that looked like it had been folded a hundred times.

"The insert says that it's chemically related to the narcotic meperidine. It's a class-five narcotic and an anti-peristaltic agent. It also warns that overdoses may lead to respiratory depression, coma or death."

"Can you put that in English?" Dan asked.

"It stops your gut from pushing things through, and an over-dose suppresses your breathing until you go to sleep and die."

"How many did Ted take out of stock?"

"I don't know for sure," she replied. "Maybe twenty-five or thirty. That's enough for one every six hours for six days."

"Would that be enough to kill a two-hundred pound woman if she got it all in one dose?"

Grace shrugged. "They don't give information like that. I'd have to guess it would be. That's thirty times the recommended dose." Grace's eyes grew wide with recognition. "Is that how he killed Jean?"

Dan shook his head, "No. Jean was killed by a small incision in her neck that cut the artery to her brain. Ann Olsen was attacked and Ted packed her rectum with little white pills that were a barbiturate. I'll ask the lab to see if it was Lomotil, but I'm sure that was it."

"My God! I just can't believe it?" Grace said, shivering. "He just never … seemed like …"

"We found the cover to Jean's planner inside the wood stove in Ted's garage, and hairs in the boat and freezer. Could he have stored Jean's body in the freezer without you knowing?"

Grace looked at Dan in Horror. "I *never* look in that freezer," she said emphatically. "Ted stores body parts and carcasses in there all the time. I don't even want to think about what's in there, much less looking at it."

"Can you tell me anything about Ted's relationship with his wife, Emily?"

"There's nothing much to tell. They were individuals. She did her thing upstairs, in the house, and he did his thing downstairs, here in the office. They were nice to each other, and I never heard them fight, if that's what you mean ... but I don't think I ever saw Emily down here more than twice in the eleven years I've worked for Ted."

"Ted said that Emily wanted to divorce him. He thought he'd lose the clinic if she did."

"Well, that sounds possible. I think Emily hated this clinic. I think that it irritated her that Ted spent so much time here. Towards the end I think she kinda gave up trying to drag him away. I know sometimes she even ate alone while Ted was down here doing something."

"I read the doctor's report from the emergency room when Emily was brought in," Dan said. "The report said she was suffering from an allergic reaction to a penicillin shot. The report also said that Ted had given her a shot of epinephrine here before bringing her into the hospital. Would you have noticed if you were missing some from stock?"

"Probably not, but we don't use much. We only stock a couple of vials at any time, so I would've had to reorder. Hang on a second." She disappeared into the back and Dan could hear metal file drawers opening and closing.

"I grabbed all the invoices from ninety-eight and ninety nine." Grace leafed through them. "I ordered epinephrine in January, before she died, then again in October. If he had used much I would have reordered it sooner. It couldn't have been epinephrine that he gave her."

Williams nodded. "Is there anything extraordinary that you

ordered right after her death?"

Grace leafed through the stack again. "No, just the normal stuff. Lots of antibiotics. Lots of vaccines."

"Penicillin?" Dan asked.

She looked through the stack again. "Some." She froze. "You don't think Ted gave her more penicillin instead of epinephrine?"

"What's worse than giving more of what she's allergic to?" Dan asked.

Grace's eyes filled with tears. "That's terrible."

. . .

Williams was awaiting his appointment in the doctor's office in the Pine City clinic. The cover story in the June issue of *Field and Stream* was bass fishing. He was weighing the value of crank baits against plastic worms when Dr. Glen Bergstrom walked in.

"Wow!" Bergstrom exclaimed, looking at Dan's bruised cheek. "Heard about Ted Gapinski. Is there a connection?" He fingered the bruised cheek.

"Dammit!" Dan complained. "Why do you always have to poke the places that already hurt?"

Bergstrom smiled. "Professional curiosity. We doctors have to know how bad things hurt."

Williams rubbed the sore cheek. "We had a chase last night and I plowed the Ford into a ditch."

"Good thing you had your seat belt on," Bergstrom said as he made a note in Dan's file. "Did anyone examine you last night?"

"I had x-rays until I glowed. Nothing was broken, just lots of bruises."

Bergstrom leafed through the reports in the chart. "What did you think of the new endoscope at the hospital?"

"It was great," Dan replied sarcastically. "Like swallowing a five-eighths inch rope with a knot on the end."

"Glad you enjoyed it. Maybe we'll have to make it a regular visit." The young doctor had a big smile. "But it did give us some good news. You don't have an ulcer."

"Sally will be so relieved. But, why does my belly burn?"

"Maybe a little indigestion, or maybe a little weakness in the hiatal sphincter. Does it get worse in the spring?"

"I think so," Dan replied.

"How about after you drink coffee?"

"Yes."

"After drinking liquor?"

"Yes."

"Then cut back on those things in the spring," Bergstrom said. "Those are all pretty classic symptoms of acid reflux."

"Should I give up sex too?" Dan asked.

Bergstrom lowered the chart and frowned. "I don't know why you'd have to."

"Because that's the only other thing that I enjoy. I thought you'd want to make it a clean sweep."

"Naw," Bergstrom said with a smile. "I wouldn't want your prostate to get congested. Do you take antacids?"

"Now and then. Sooner. Later. I should own stock in Tums."

"Tums are okay," Bergstrom said, "but the liquids are generally more effective."

"Liquids tend to stain the pocket of my shirt."

"Smart ass."

"That's the biggest compliment you've ever given me."

Bergstrom smiled. "I'll give you some Zantac samples. Try them for a month. If they work, let me know and I'll call in a prescription." Bergstrom stood to leave.

"Wait a second, doc. I've got a question for you."

Bergstrom sat back down. "What is it?"

"Last night, Ted Gapinski admitted to me before he died that he'd killed his wife, Emily. I read the report at the hospital and it says she died of an allergic reaction to a penicillin shot."

"Hmm, interesting. I assume that they gave her shots of epinephrine and Benadryl in the emergency room?"

"Not initially," Dan said. "Ted told them Emily had taken oral Benadryl and later he'd given her epinephrine at home, from his veterinary stock of pharmaceuticals. His assistant checked his drug orders and she says they didn't use any epinephrine the week Emily died. When Emily got to the hospital she was getting worse fast. They said she had rupturing blood cells and a respiratory collapse that lead to a cardiac arrest." Williams took a deep breath. "Well, if he didn't give her epinephrine, it was something else that made it worse. Like another shot of penicillin. The vet clinic orders it by the pound, and they don't track usage."

"More penicillin would have been very bad," Bergstrom said. "On the other hand, some veterinary antibiotics are lethal to humans. It could have been any of them."

"How about vaccines?"

"I'm not much of an expert, but I'd guess that even a massive dose of something like a bovine brucellosis vaccine could be lethal to a human."

"Well," Dan said, "thanks for helping to deepen the mystery."

"You know, Dan, penicillin, come to think of it, would be perfect. It's cheap, and the clerk wouldn't miss a human-sized dose. If someone demanded an autopsy, they would expect to find penicillin in her body anyway. I guess it's a moot point now that Ted's dead, but you could nail it down by exhuming the body and doing some testing."

"Can't," Dan replied. "Ted had her cremated within hours of her death. The perfect crime."

Bergstrom shook his head.

. . .

Dan drove to Moose Lake and parked in front of the dime store. Through the window he could see Ann Olsen ringing up a purchase at the register. He walked in and shopped around the shelves until the store was empty.

"Deputy Williams!" Ann said. "I thought I saw you poking around back here. What can I do for you?"

They walked together to the front of the store, near the cash register. "I assume that you heard about Ted Gapinski?"

Ann nodded. "Someone said that he was killed in a car accident near Kerrick."

"He committed suicide," Dan said. "Just before he died, he told me had killed Jean."

"Ted Gapinski was Jean's secret lover? I would never have

guessed. But, why would Ted want to kill Jean?" she asked.

"Jean was trying to get her baby back from the adoptive parents. Ted was the father and she thought that he'd help her, then marry her."

"So that's what she was talking about! But, the adoptive parents would never give the child back, would they?"

"We all know that," Dan agreed. "I suppose that's why Jean was trying to convince Ted to help her kidnap the baby. He said that she got crazy, and he killed her."

"Oh, Lord. She was that hung up on it." Ann shook her head in disbelief.

"I have a question for you," Dan said. "It relates to a different crime. Who brought the gonorrhea epidemic into the group?"

"We were never sure. It could have been a number of people. We suspected that it was that ass, Orrin Petrich."

"Could it have been Ted?" Dan asked.

"Might have been. If I rule out all the people that were never with anyone except Jeanie, their wives, or me, it's down to about three or four. Ted would be one of them."

Ann snapped her fingers. "Of course it was Ted! Everyone else is pretty much local. A big trip for most of us is to Duluth. But Ted was always going off to these conventions for veterinarians in Las Vegas and San Francisco. His wife always stayed at home, I guess. When he came back he'd tell Jean and me how he was the life of the party and never went to any of the sessions."

"Ted said that Emily wanted a divorce and he'd lose the clinic if it happened," Dan explained. "I think he transmitted the gonorrhea knowingly to Emily as a way to get her to take a penicillin shot, which eventually killed her.

"My God" Ann said. "But, divorce is a pretty thin reason to kill somebody."

"He almost killed you for less."

Ann's face turned ashen. "Ted beat me up? But why?"

"He must have learned from Jean that she'd been confiding in you. After he killed her, he had to silence you to cover the trail. He tried to make it look like a botched burglary, and he hoped you wouldn't be found until after the pills he stuffed in you were absorbed, and you were dead. Thanks to you and your phone call, things didn't quite go as he had planned."

A visible chill ran over Ann, like she had just seen a ghost walk into the room. "That's spooky. But I didn't know about Ted and Jean."

"But Ted didn't know that," Dan said. "I've got another mystery, too. Did Jean ever talk about Carl Johnson?"

"He was the one that hurt her a couple of times," Ann said without hesitation.

"Well, that confirms what Jean's planner said. One, two, and three strikes. Do you know what happened to him?"

Ann shrugged. "I haven't seen him in years. Is he still around?"

"I checked the old records at the courthouse," Dan replied. "He'd been in trouble quite a few times. It ended in ninety-eight. I called Carl Senior. It seems that Junior disappeared on a canoe trip with a couple of the guys from the group. The official story is that he went fishing alone early one morning and the wind came up. The others found the canoe washed up on the windward shore. They reported that he drowned. Do you know otherwise?"

Ann shook her head. " That'd be murder. Jean said the guys policed themselves. I would have doubted that it ever came to that, but now, from what you've told me, I guess I wouldn't be surprised."

"I think that there was a lot more that went on with Jean's customers than will ever come to light," said Dan. "I called the Lake County sheriff's office. They're going to talk to the park service, but there's a hundred-thousand acres of wilderness up there. I'd be surprised if they ever find a body. We've leaned on the guys who were on the trip, but they've got a pat story and no one has cracked."

Ann opened her mouth, but no word came out. She composed herself, stared at her hands and tried again. "I got a call yesterday, from a lawyer in Hinckley. He said he knew you."

"Was his name Peikert?" Dan asked.

"Yeah, that was the name. Is he on the level?"

"He's a real lawyer, if that's what you mean."

"I mean, is he ... was he really Jean's lawyer?"

"It seems that he was," Dan said. "He was doing work for her. Why do you ask?"

"He can't locate Jeanie's baby," Ann replied. "The adoptive parents divorced and moved out of Minnesota. The mother had custody of the girl, and she must've remarried. He can't get the new name. He's given up searching."

"So he wanted you to help?" Dan asked."You thought she had

an abortion."

"The lawyer says Jeanie put me in her will. I get all her stuff, if he can't find the baby."

Williams smiled. "That's pretty nice of her. You seemed to be her only friend, Ann. Even her family had abandoned her. I guess it makes sense."

"Some good friend I was. I told her to confront the guy. I got her killed."

"Ann," Dan said, "you weren't responsible for what happened to Jean and Ted. They created their own little fantasy worlds that led to their ends. Take your baby to Disneyland. That's what Jean would have wanted. You'll be living her dream after all."

Tears appeared in Ann's eyes. "Maybe you're right," she said. "I'll think about it."

ABOUT THE AUTHOR

Dean Hovey is a Minnesota-based free lance writer. His writing experience includes articles for newspapers, periodicals and technical writing projects. He is the author of another mystery published by j-Press, *Where Evil Hides*. His education includes Bachelor's and Master's degrees in three fields, including engineering and biology. He has traveled extensively in North America and is an amateur history buff. He contends that there is no better place to study people under stress than at an airport. Hobbies include: hunting, reading, gourmet cooking, fishing, travel, and people watching. Attention to detail is one of his hallmarks. His proofreaders include a retired deputy sheriff, a registered nurse, an archeologist, and a computer programmer who provide critical comments on technical details and direction on plot. Hovey is a voracious mystery reader, and some of his favorite authors include: Patricia Cornwell, Tony Hillerman, Tom Clancy, Faye Kellerman, and Dick Francis. He brings Minnesota natural history and local culture to his books like Hillerman does for the Arizona Navajo reservation, with the technical details of Patricia Cornwell.

If you liked *Hooker* you'll also like:

WHERE EVIL HIDES

by

Dean Hovey

$12.95

ISBN: 0-966011-8-x

Available thru:

j-Press Publishing

4796 N. 126th St.

White Bear Lake, MN 55110

Phone 888-407-1723

Fax: 651-429-1819

Website: http://www.jpresspublishing.com

email: sjackson@jpresspublishing.com

Also available in your local bookstore